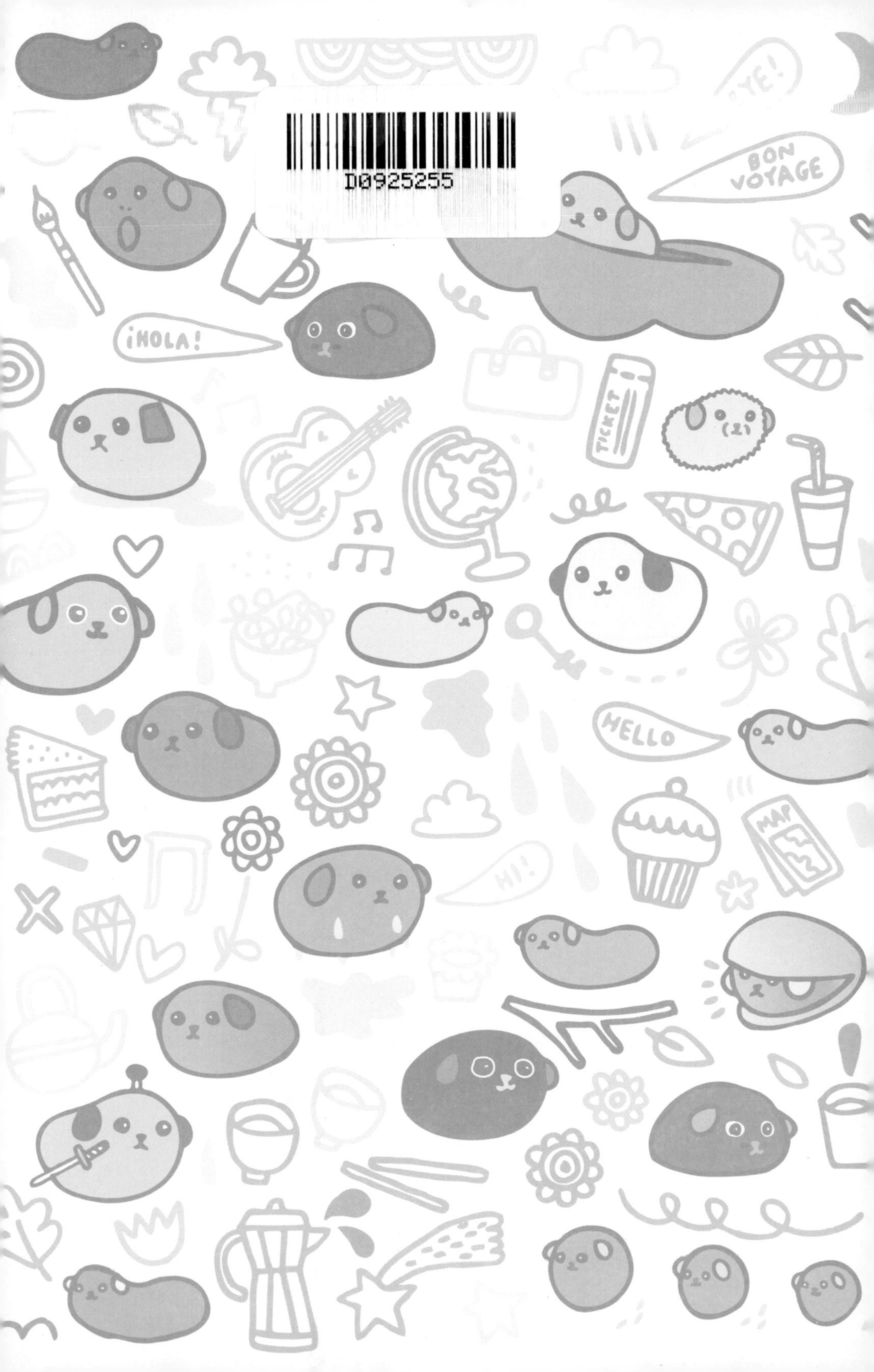
BYE!
BON VOYAGE
¡HOLA!
TICKET
HELLO
HI!
MAP

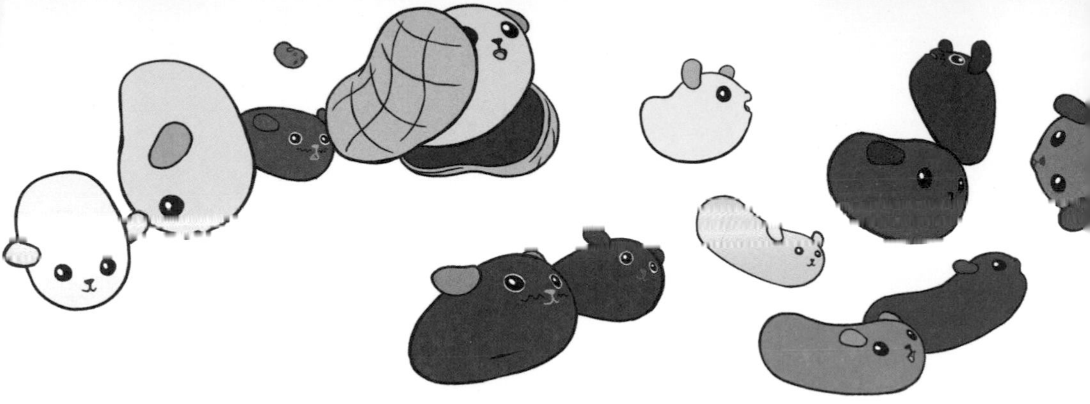

mameshiba

On the LOOSE!

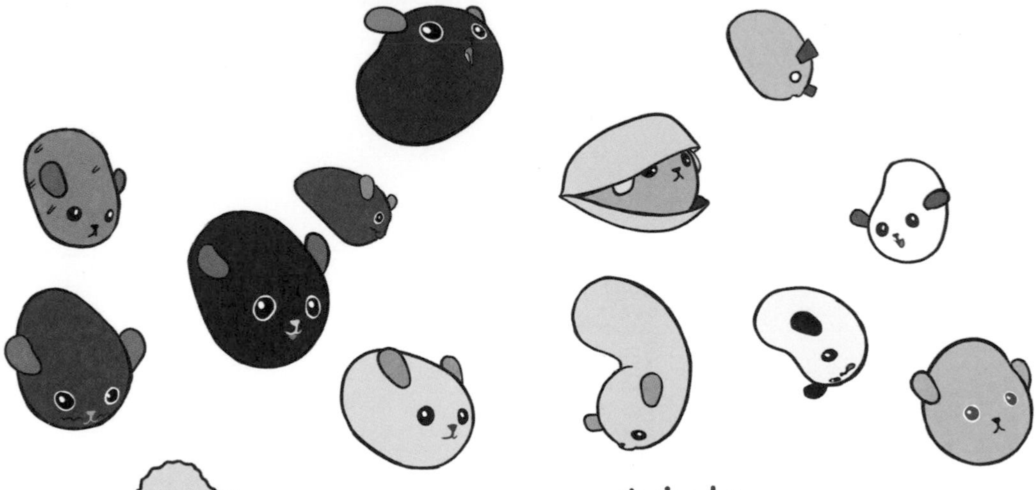

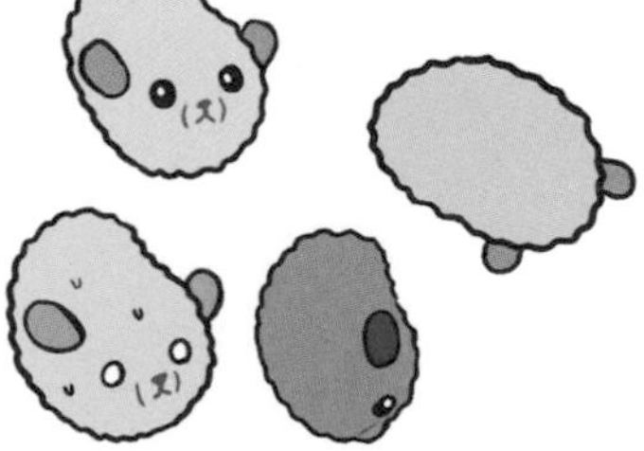

stories by
james turner

art by
jorge monlongo

"Mameshiba Shorts" by
gemma correll

Mameshiba:
On the Loose!

Stories by **James Turner**
Art by **Jorge Monlongo**
"Mameshiba Shorts" by **Gemma Correll**

Cover Art • **Jorge Monlongo**
Graphics and Cover Design • **Fawn Lau**
Editor • **Traci N. Todd**
Original Mameshiba character
creation and design • **Sukwon Kim**
Original Mameshiba
art direction • **Shoko Watanabe**

Special thanks to Chris Duffy for his support and guidance.

The stories, characters and incidents mentioned in this
publication are entirely fictional.

Printed in China

Published by VIZ Media, LLC
P.O. Box 77010
San Francisco, CA 94107

10 9 8 7 6 5 4 3 2 1
First printing, July 2011

www.vizkids.com

www.viz.com

PARENTAL ADVISORY
MAMESHIBA: ON THE LOOSE!
is rated A and is suitable for
readers of all ages.
ratings.viz.com

Table of CONTENTS

What are Mameshiba?

Simply put, *mameshiba* means "bean dog" in Japanese. But Mameshiba aren't beans or dogs. They're a little bit of both! And the one thing these bean dogs like more than anything else is trivia. So if you ever see a Mameshiba and it asks, "Did you know?" listen up. Because you're about to hear something very special.

Edamame

Edamame is the brave, determined leader of the pack.

The Jelly Beans

The Jelly Beans are a colorful crew from America.

Peanut

Peanut likes to try new things and always thinks outside the shell.

Lentil

Lentil is aware of everything that's going on and is passionate about facts and figures.

The Green Peas

Truly like peas in a pod, these three hate to be alone.

Chickpea

Chickpea hates to be left out and can be a wee bit self-involved.

Black Soybean

Black soybean is the athlete of the bunch.

Sword Bean

Sword Bean is an honest and loyal companion.

Sweet Beans

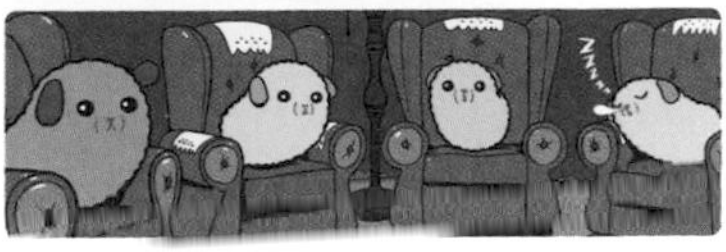

The sweetbeans are very old and very wise.

Pistachio

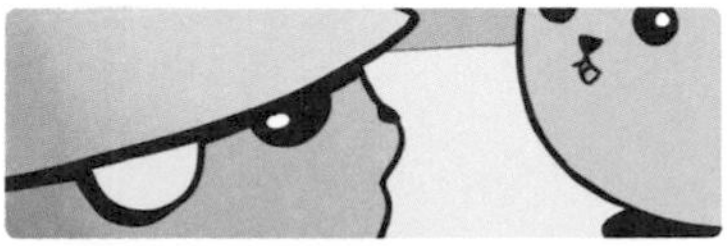

Pistachio is the quiet, hide-in-the-shell type.

Chili Bean

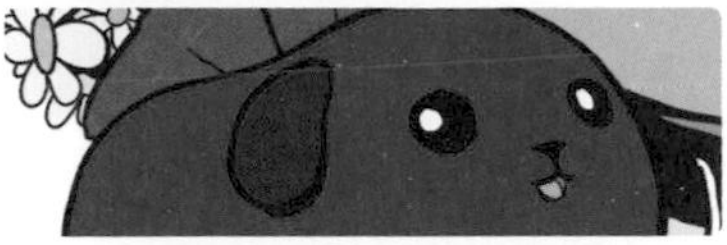

Chili Bean is a true romantic.

Almond

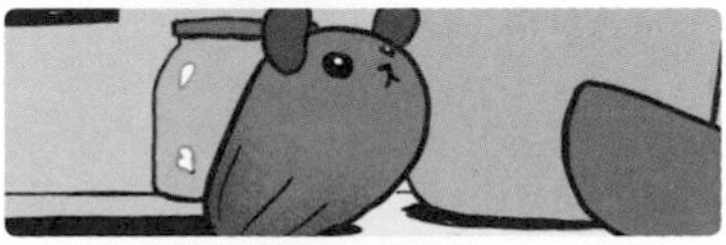

Almond's a bit uptight and is Cocoa Bean's best friend.

Natto

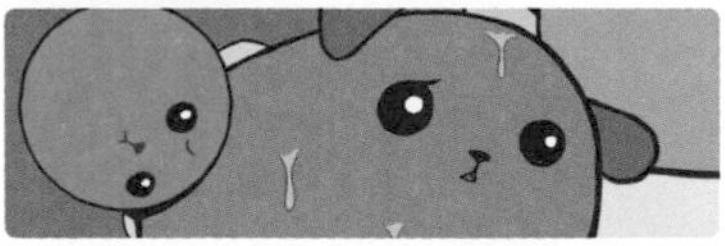

Natto always sticks to its guns. And just about everything else.

Black-eyed Pea

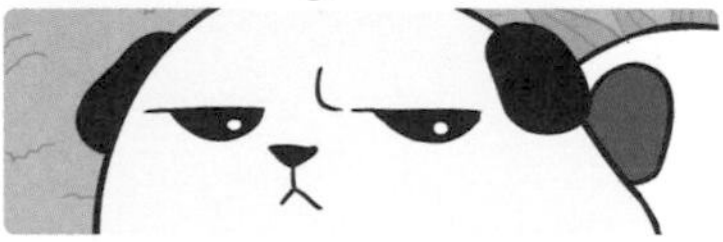

Black-eyed Pea is a cool legume with a very dry sense of humor.

Black Bean

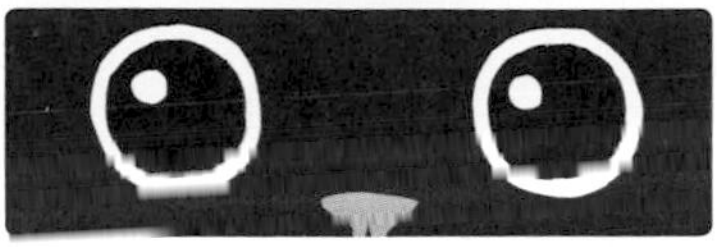

Black Bean is very shy and has perfected the fine art of staring.

Tiger Bean

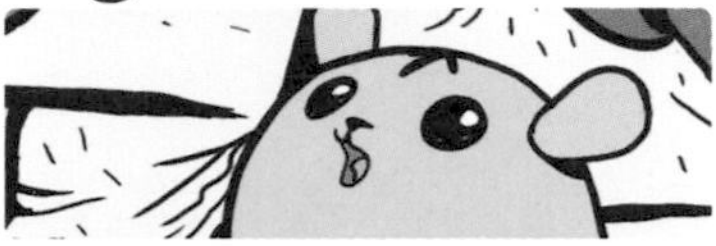

Tiger is a forgetful little bean who can sometimes be a bit selfish.

White Soybean

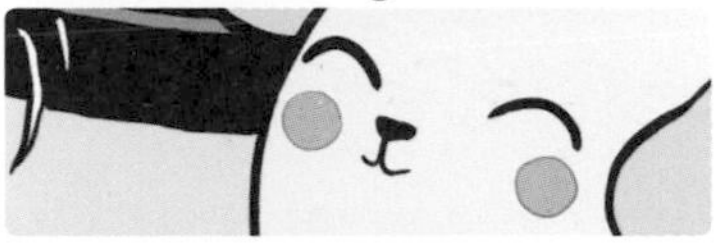

White Soybean's heart is pure and true.

Cocoa Bean

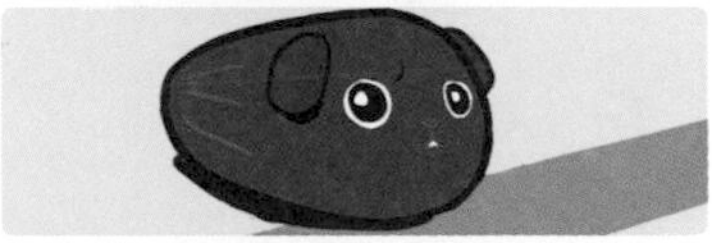

Cocoa has a wide-eyed, innocent view of the world.

Cranberry Bean

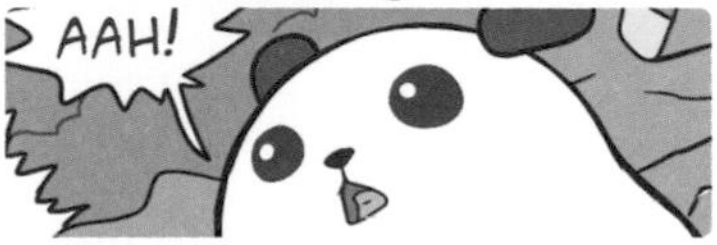
AAH!

Cranberry is very competitive and wants to be the best at everything.

The Scream

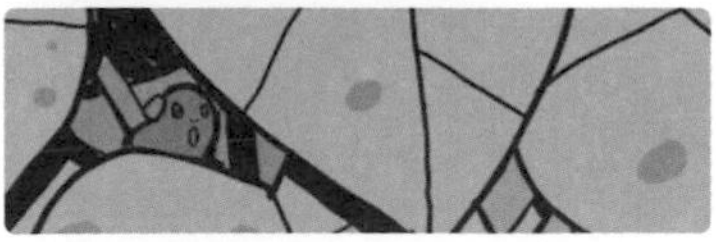

This mysterious bean is rarely ever seen, but it's hiding in this book. Can you find it?

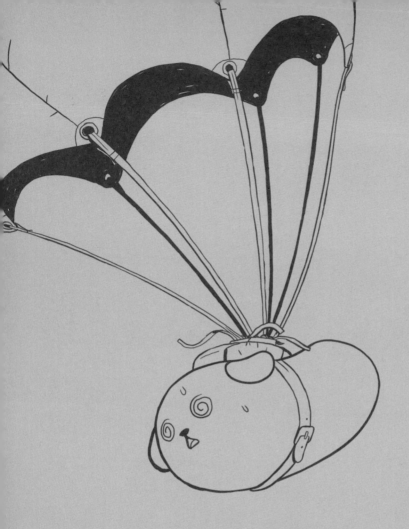

mameshiba

On the LOOSE!

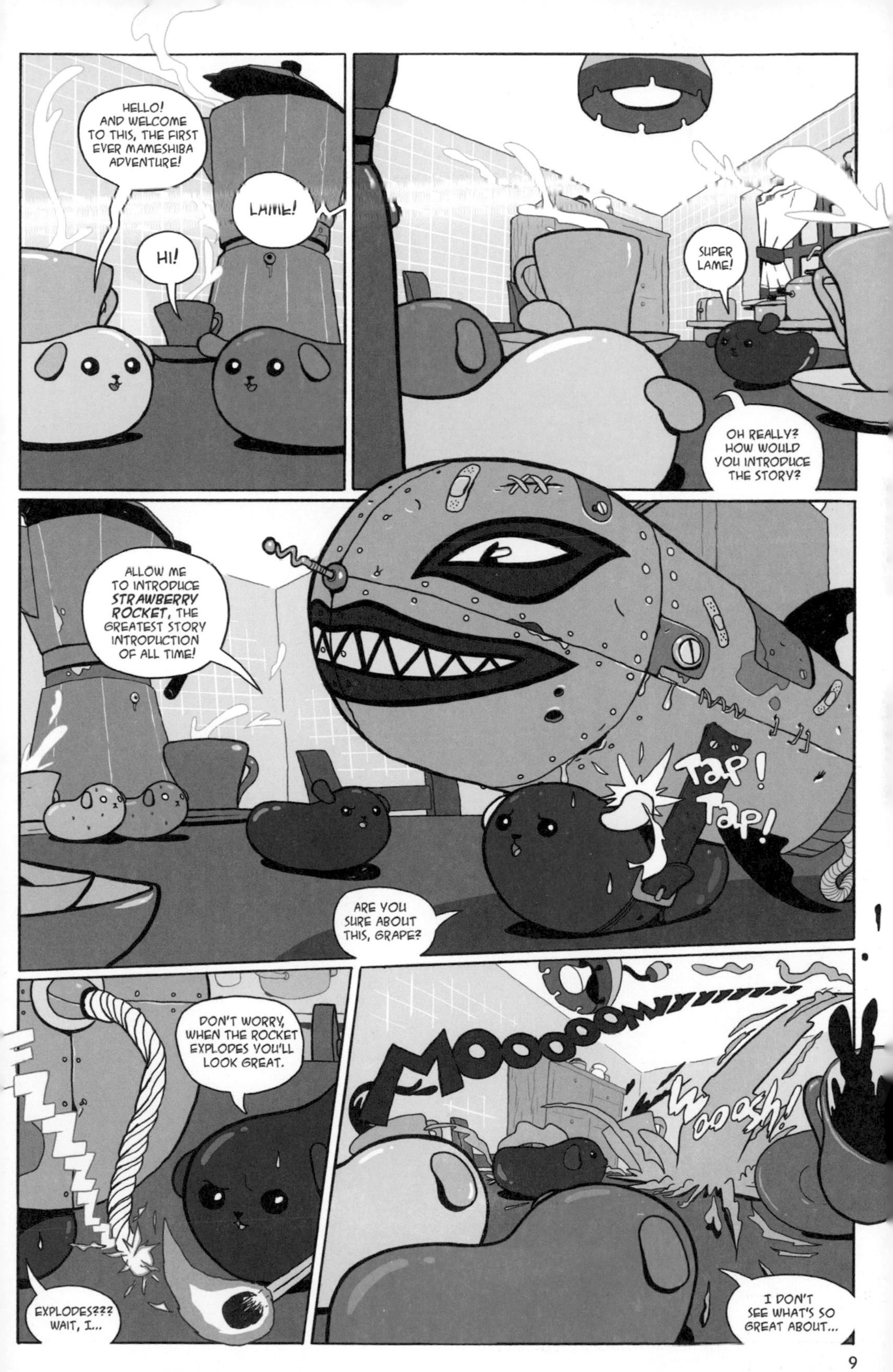
HELLO! AND WELCOME TO THIS, THE FIRST EVER MAMESHIBA ADVENTURE!
HI!
LAME!
SUPER LAME!
OH REALLY? HOW WOULD YOU INTRODUCE THE STORY?
ALLOW ME TO INTRODUCE **STRAWBERRY ROCKET**, THE GREATEST STORY INTRODUCTION OF ALL TIME!
TAP! TAP!
ARE YOU SURE ABOUT THIS, GRAPE?
DON'T WORRY, WHEN THE ROCKET EXPLODES YOU'LL LOOK GREAT.
EXPLODES??? WAIT, I...
MOOOOOMYYYYYY
WOOOSH!
I DON'T SEE WHAT'S SO GREAT ABOUT...

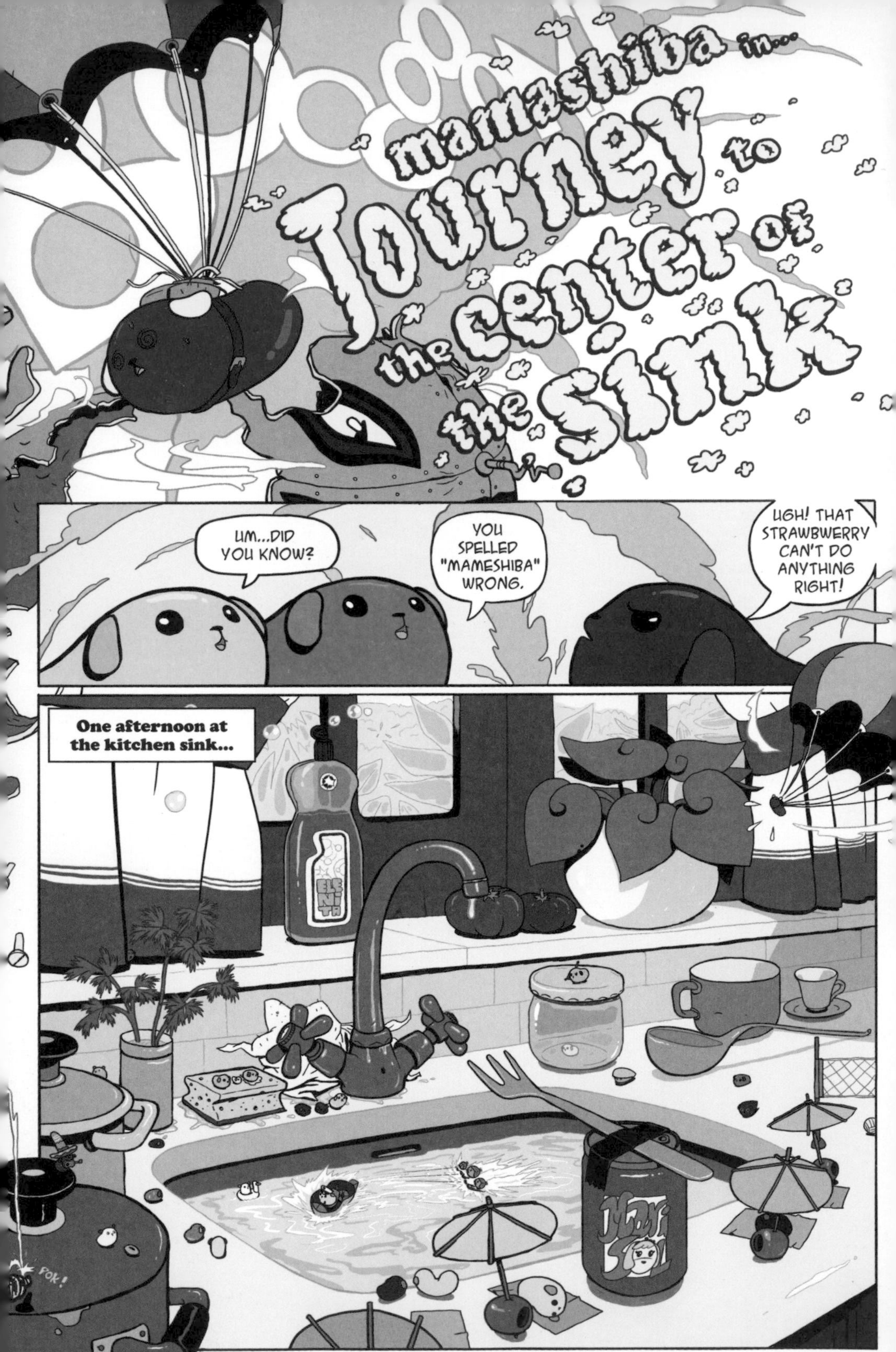
mamashiba in...
Journey to the center of the Sink
UM...DID YOU KNOW?
YOU SPELLED "MAMESHIBA" WRONG.
UGH! THAT STRAWBWERRY CAN'T DO ANYTHING RIGHT!
One afternoon at the kitchen sink...
POK!

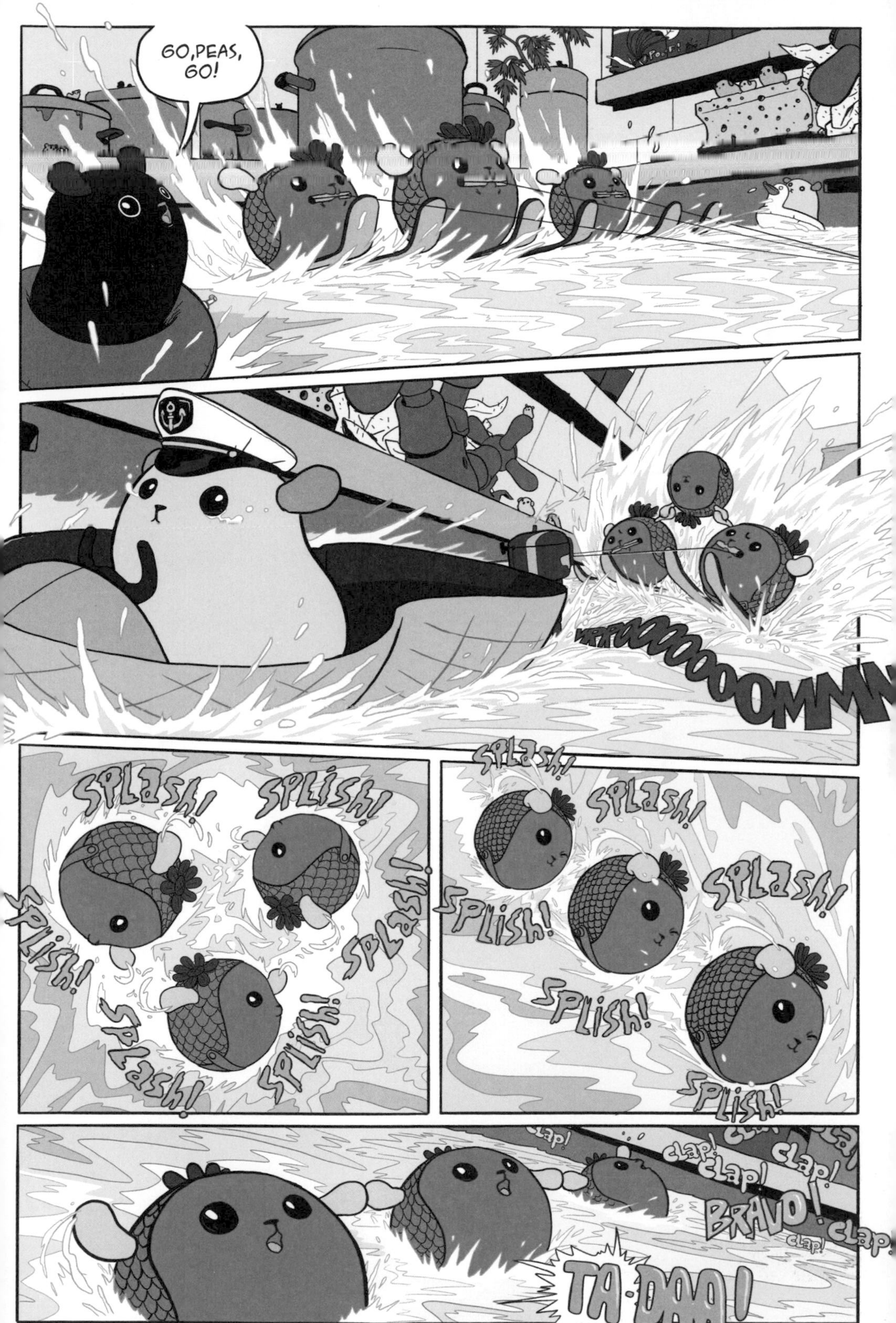

GO, PEAS, GO!
VRRROOOOOOOOOMMM
SPLASH!
SPLISH!
SPLISH!
SPLASH!
SPLASH!
SPLISH!
SPLASH!
SPLASH!
SPLISH!
SPLASH!
SPLISH!
SPLISH!
CLAP!
CLAP!
CLAP!
CLAP!
CLAP!
BRAVO!
CLAP!
CLAP!
TA-DAA!

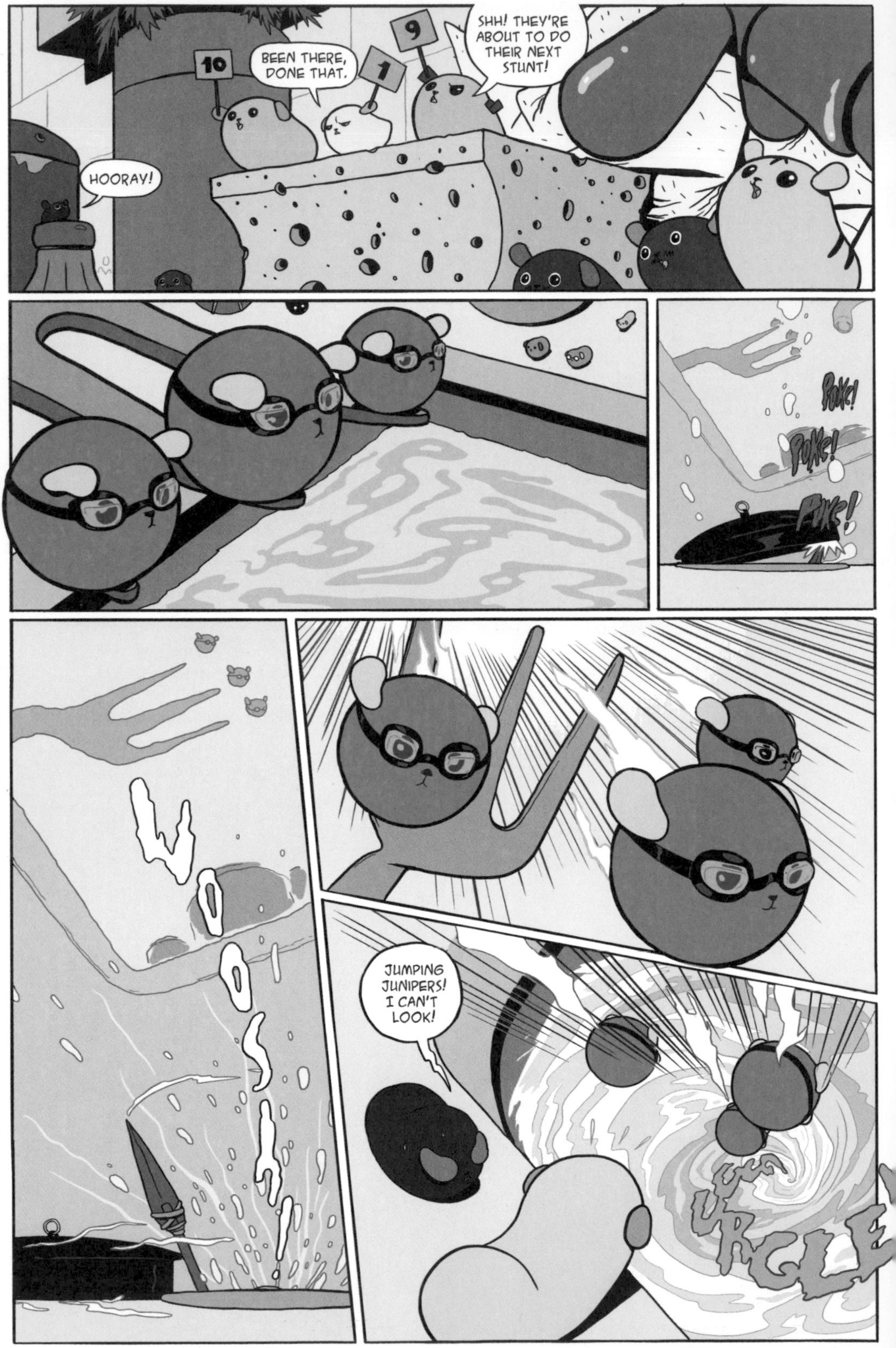
10
1
9
BEEN THERE, DONE THAT.
SHH! THEY'RE ABOUT TO DO THEIR NEXT STUNT!
HOORAY!
POKE!
POKE!
POKE!
JUMPING JUNIPERS! I CAN'T LOOK!
URGLE

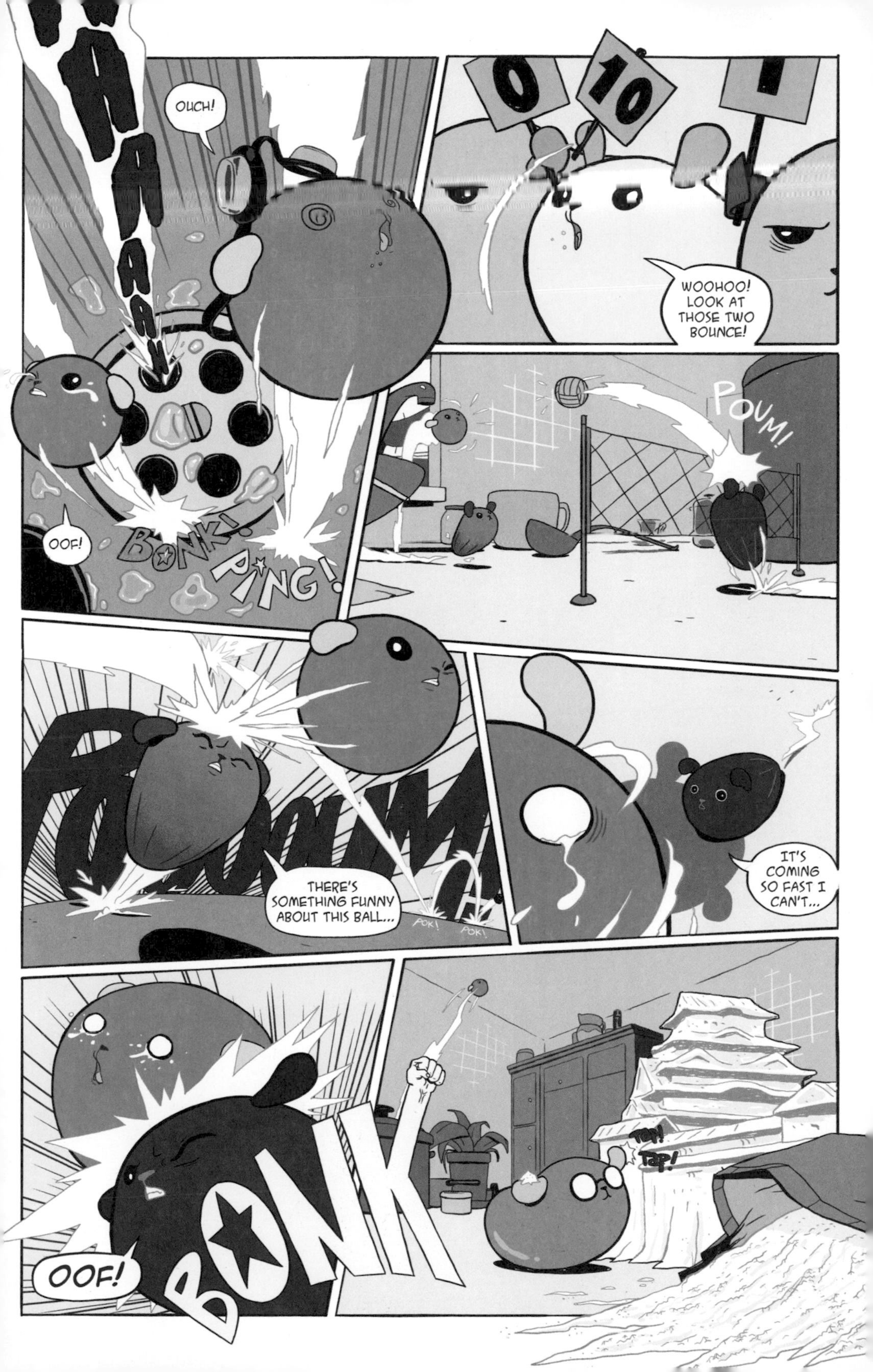
OUCH!
OOF!
BONK!
PING!
0
10
1
WOOHOO! LOOK AT THOSE TWO BOUNCE!
POUM!
THERE'S SOMETHING FUNNY ABOUT THIS BALL...
POK!
POK!
IT'S COMING SO FAST I CAN'T...
OOF!
BONK
TAP!
TAP!

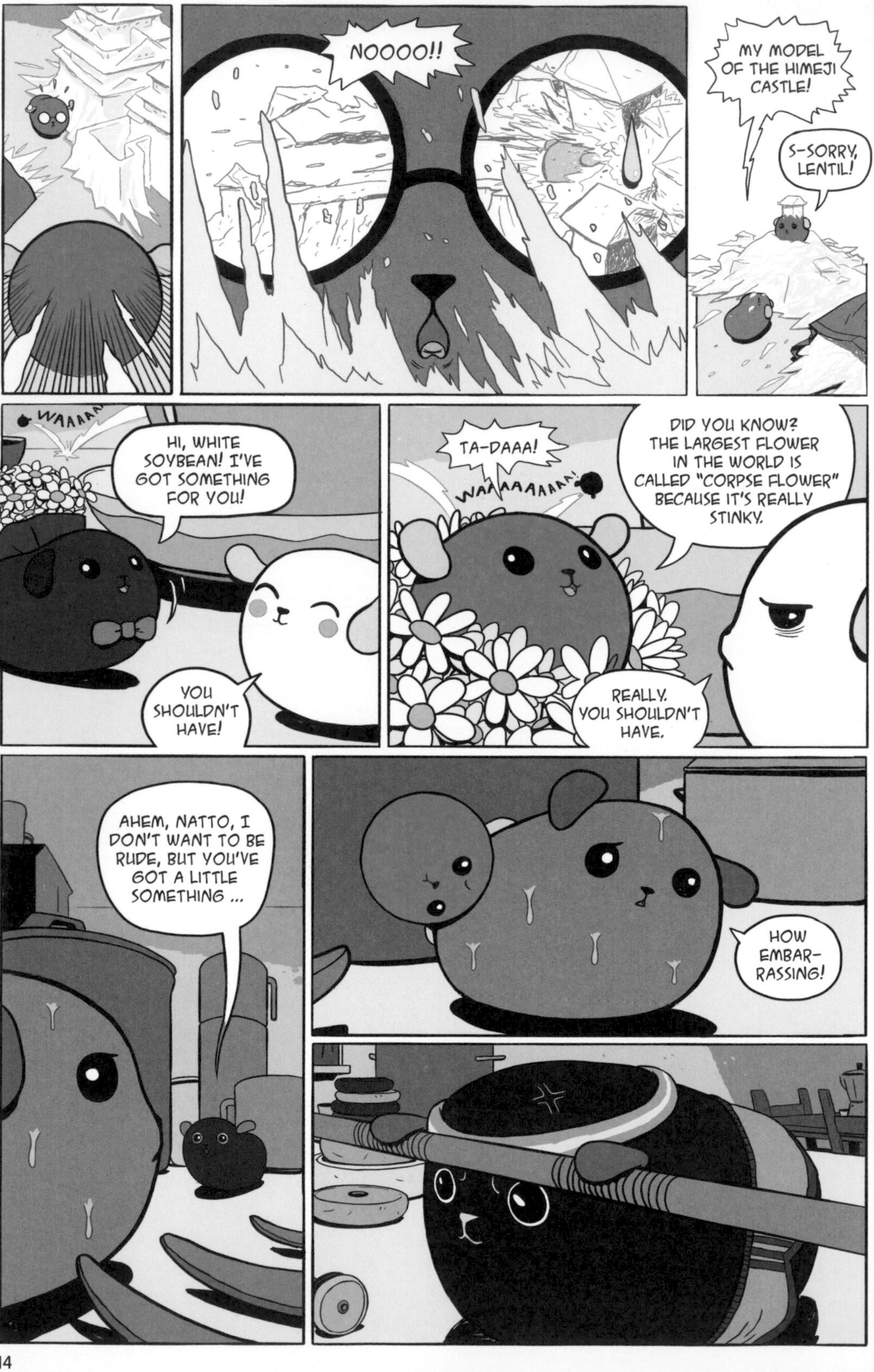
NOOOO!!
MY MODEL OF THE HIMEJI CASTLE!
S-SORRY, LENTIL!
WAAAA
HI, WHITE SOYBEAN! I'VE GOT SOMETHING FOR YOU!
YOU SHOULDN'T HAVE!
TA-DAAA!
WAAAAAAAAA!
DID YOU KNOW? THE LARGEST FLOWER IN THE WORLD IS CALLED "CORPSE FLOWER" BECAUSE IT'S REALLY STINKY.
REALLY. YOU SHOULDN'T HAVE.
AHEM, NATTO, I DON'T WANT TO BE RUDE, BUT YOU'VE GOT A LITTLE SOMETHING ...
HOW EMBAR-RASSING!

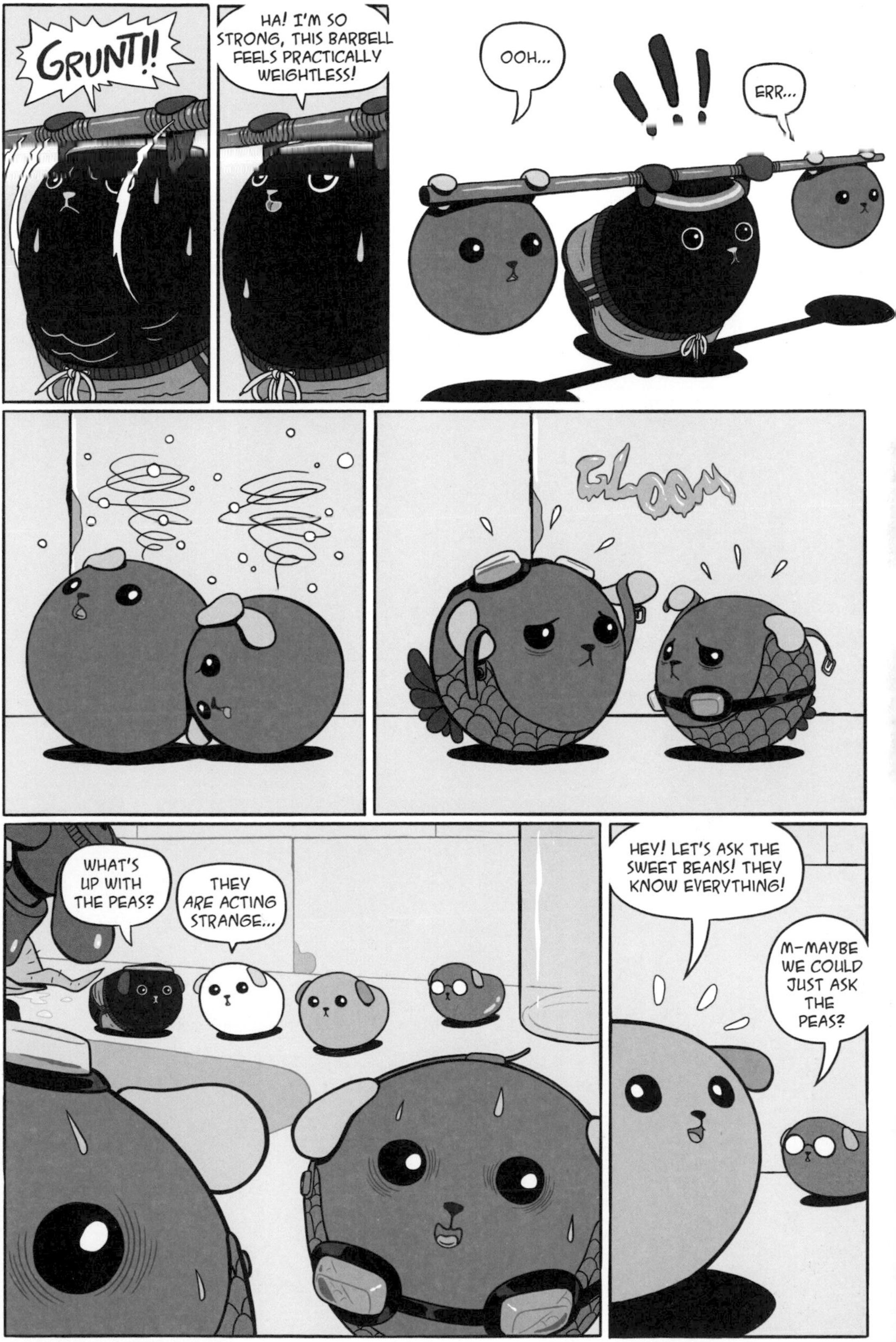
GRUNT!!
HA! I'M SO STRONG, THIS BARBELL FEELS PRACTICALLY WEIGHTLESS!
OOH...
!!!
ERR...
GLOOM
WHAT'S UP WITH THE PEAS?
THEY ARE ACTING STRANGE...
HEY! LET'S ASK THE SWEET BEANS! THEY KNOW EVERYTHING!
M-MAYBE WE COULD JUST ASK THE PEAS?

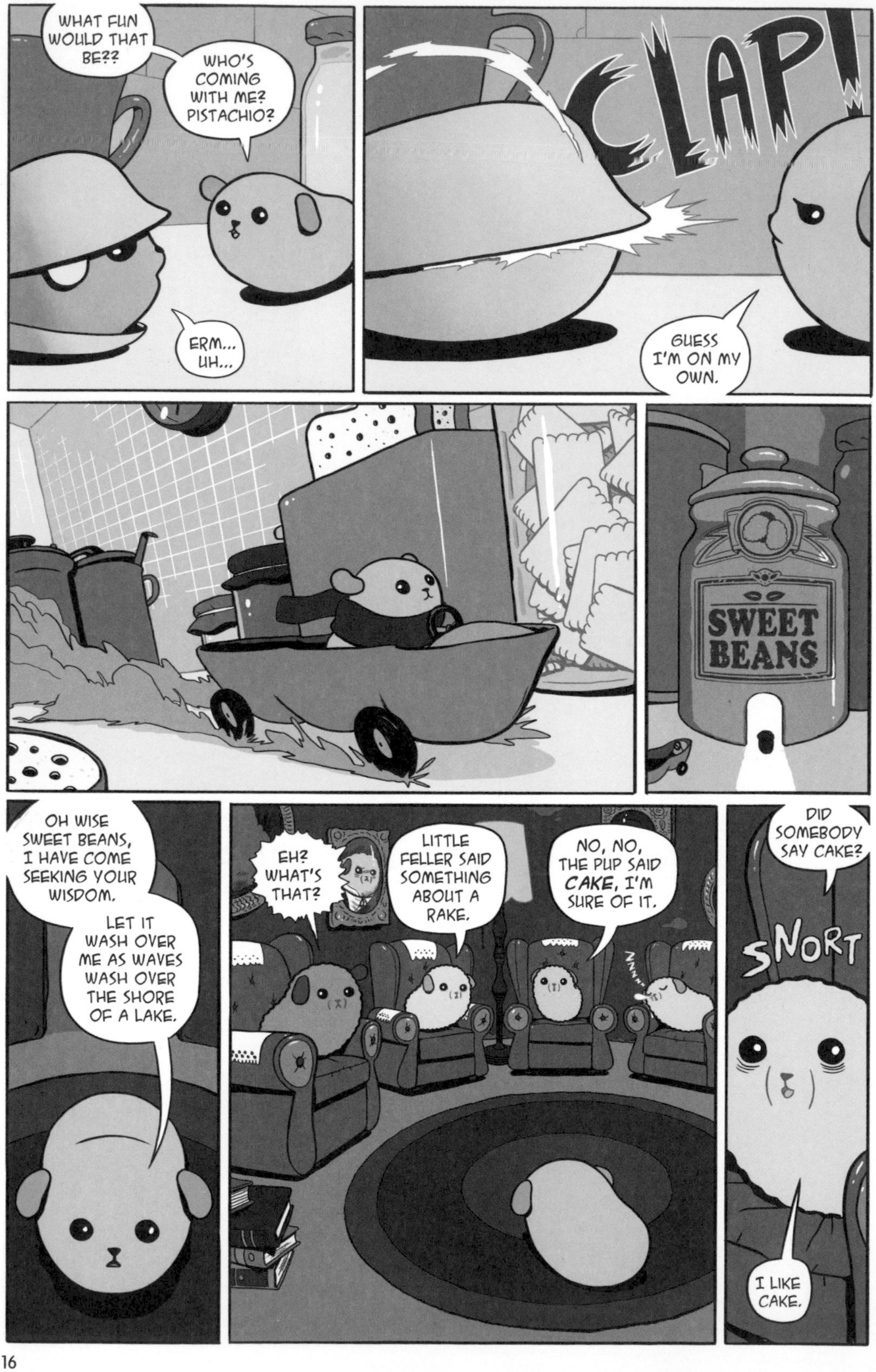

WHAT FUN WOULD THAT BE??
WHO'S COMING WITH ME? PISTACHIO?
ERM... UH...
CLAP!
GUESS I'M ON MY OWN.
SWEET BEANS
OH WISE SWEET BEANS, I HAVE COME SEEKING YOUR WISDOM.
LET IT WASH OVER ME AS WAVES WASH OVER THE SHORE OF A LAKE.
EH? WHAT'S THAT?
LITTLE FELLER SAID SOMETHING ABOUT A RAKE.
NO, NO, THE PUP SAID CAKE, I'M SURE OF IT.
DID SOMEBODY SAY CAKE?
SNORT
I LIKE CAKE.

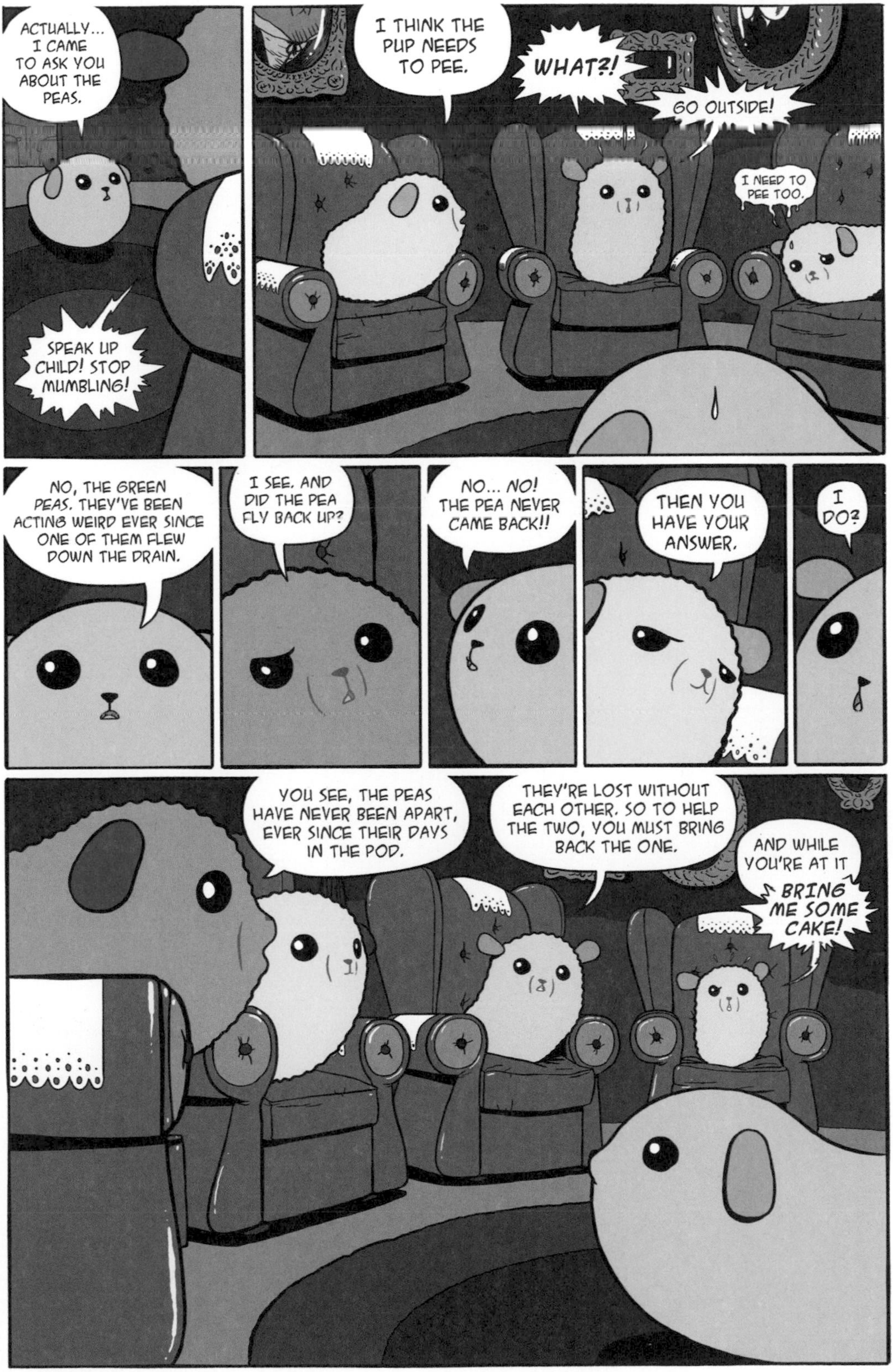
ACTUALLY... I CAME TO ASK YOU ABOUT THE PEAS.
SPEAK UP CHILD! STOP MUMBLING!
I THINK THE PUP NEEDS TO PEE.
WHAT?!
GO OUTSIDE!
I NEED TO PEE TOO.
NO, THE GREEN PEAS. THEY'VE BEEN ACTING WEIRD EVER SINCE ONE OF THEM FLEW DOWN THE DRAIN.
I SEE. AND DID THE PEA FLY BACK UP?
NO... NO! THE PEA NEVER CAME BACK!!
THEN YOU HAVE YOUR ANSWER.
I DO?
YOU SEE, THE PEAS HAVE NEVER BEEN APART, EVER SINCE THEIR DAYS IN THE POD.
THEY'RE LOST WITHOUT EACH OTHER. SO TO HELP THE TWO, YOU MUST BRING BACK THE ONE.
AND WHILE YOU'RE AT IT
BRING ME SOME CAKE!

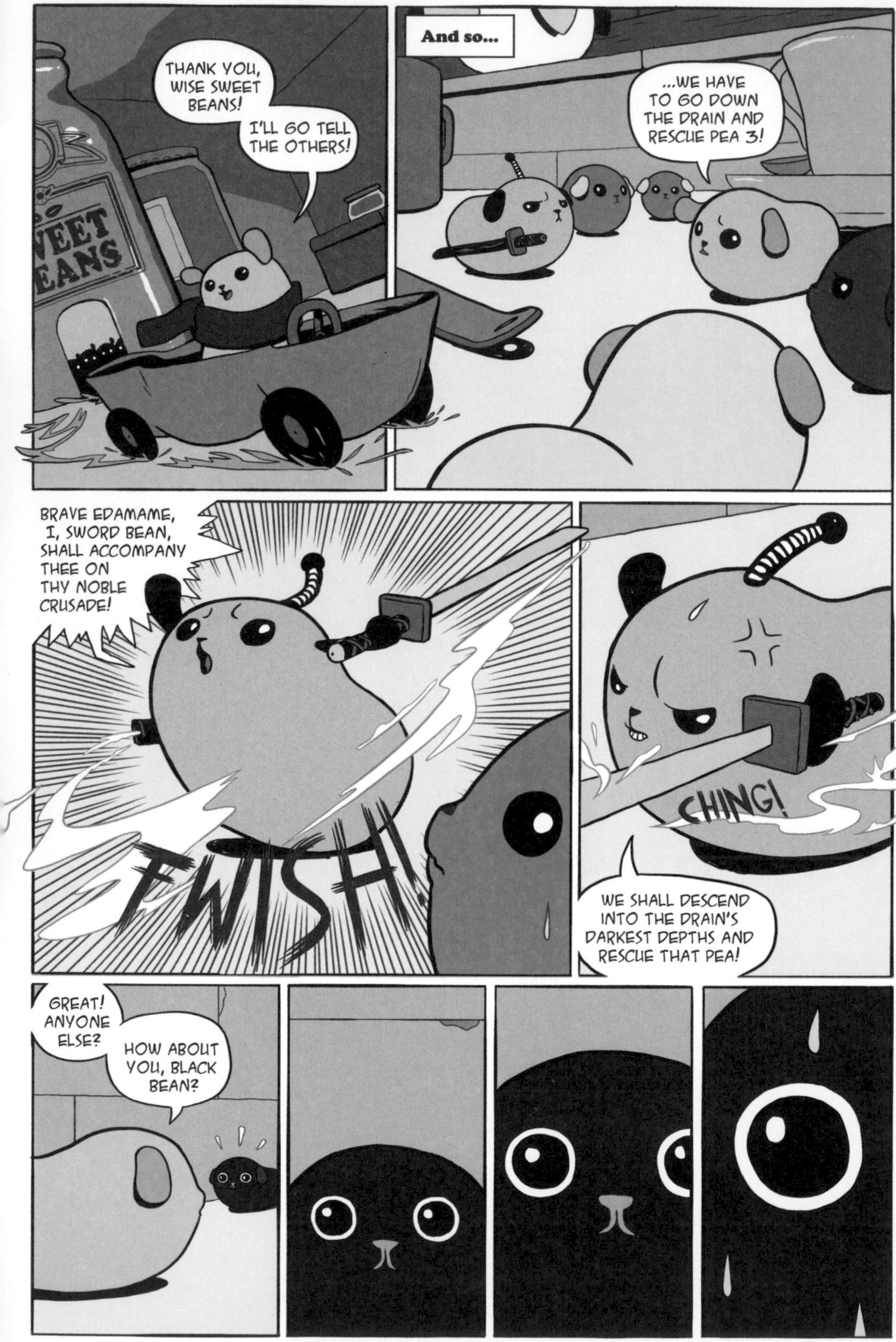
THANK YOU, WISE SWEET BEANS!
I'LL GO TELL THE OTHERS!
SWEET BEANS
And so...
...WE HAVE TO GO DOWN THE DRAIN AND RESCUE PEA 3!
BRAVE EDAMAME, I, SWORD BEAN, SHALL ACCOMPANY THEE ON THY NOBLE CRUSADE!
FWISH!
CHING!
WE SHALL DESCEND INTO THE DRAIN'S DARKEST DEPTHS AND RESCUE THAT PEA!
GREAT! ANYONE ELSE?
HOW ABOUT YOU, BLACK BEAN?

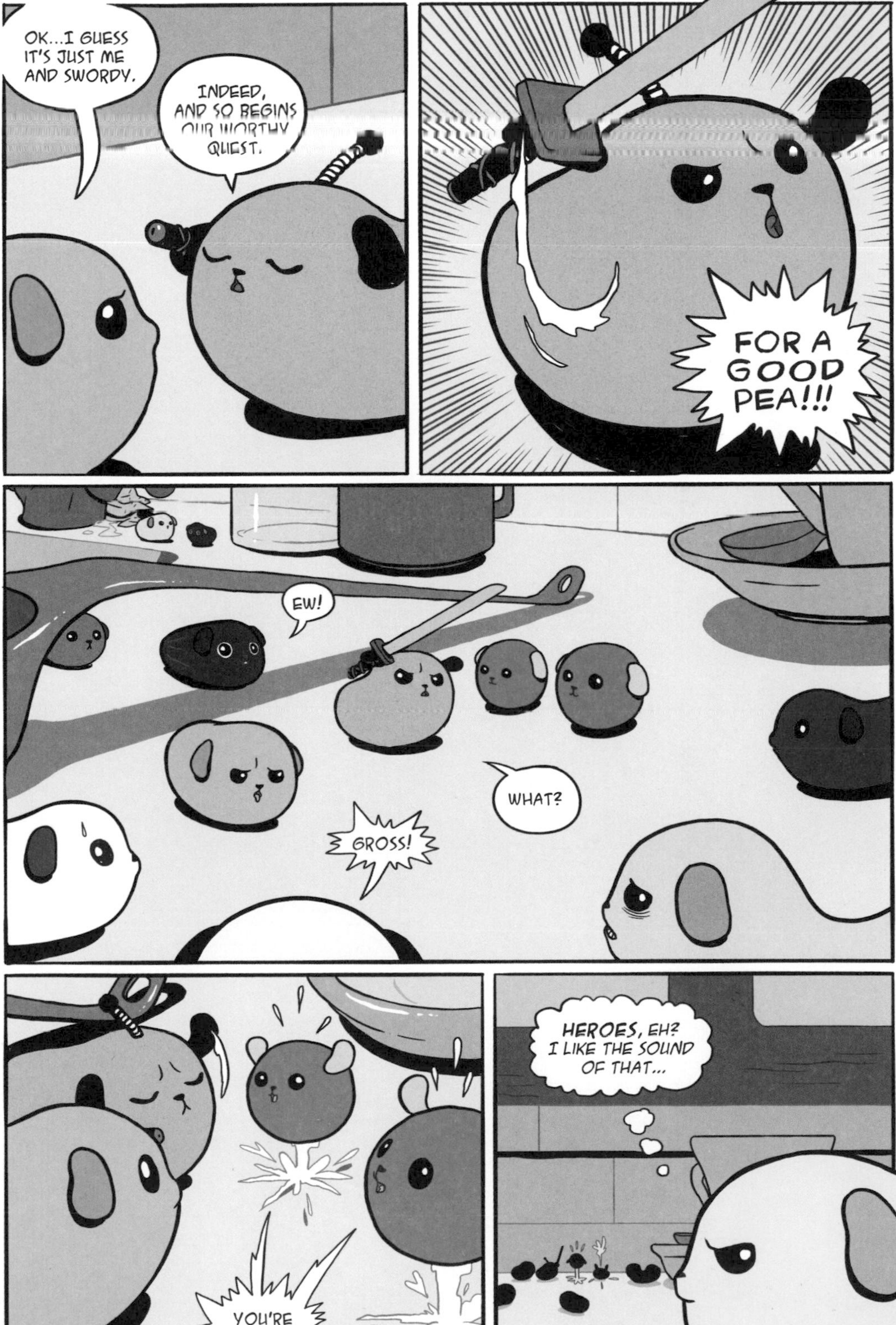
OK...I GUESS IT'S JUST ME AND SWORDY.
INDEED, AND SO BEGINS OUR WORTHY QUEST.
FOR A GOOD PEA!!!
EW!
WHAT?
GROSS!
YOU'RE OUR HEROES!!
HEROES, EH? I LIKE THE SOUND OF THAT...

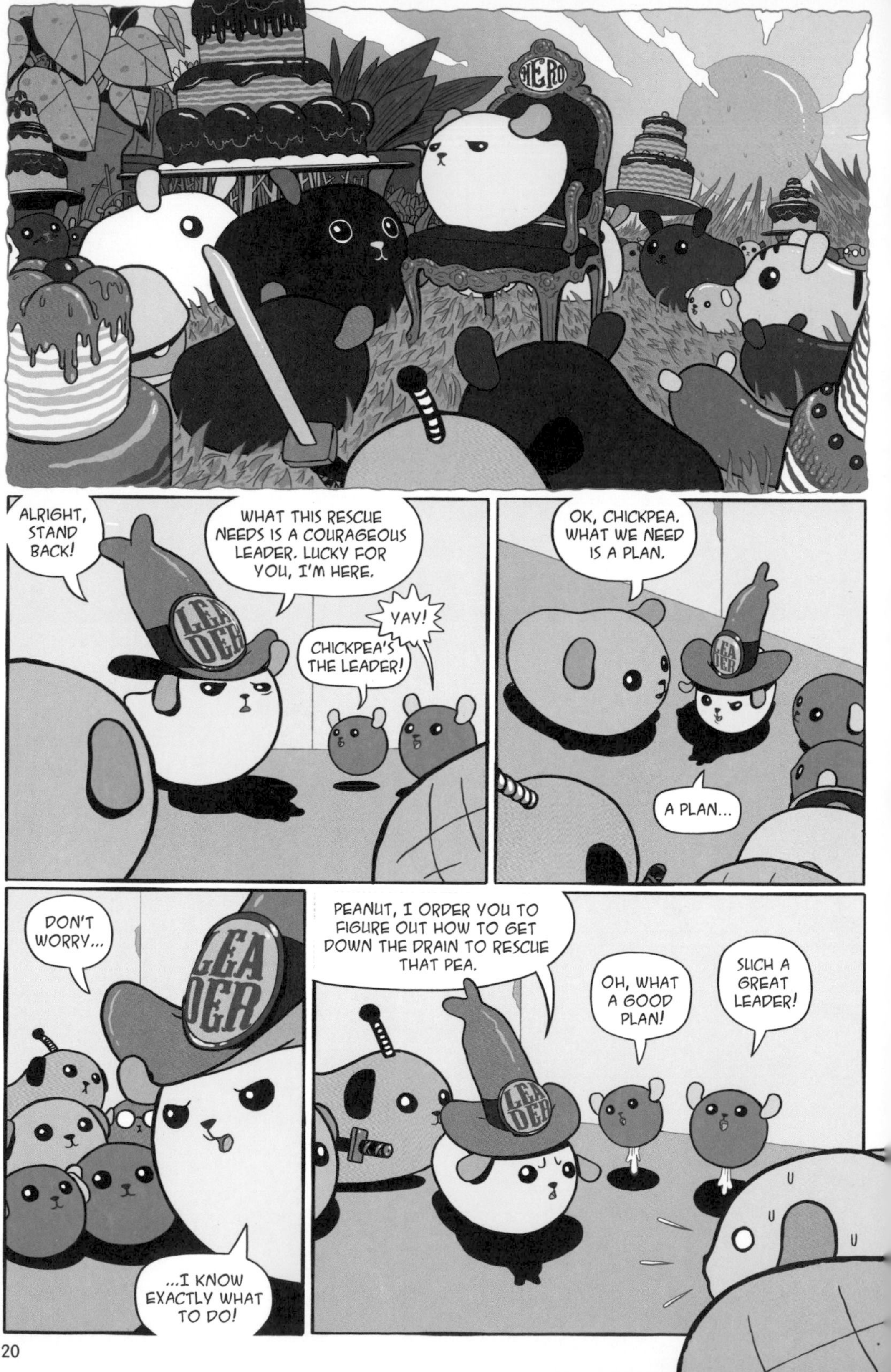
HERO
ALRIGHT, STAND BACK!
WHAT THIS RESCUE NEEDS IS A COURAGEOUS LEADER. LUCKY FOR YOU, I'M HERE.
LEADER
YAY!
CHICKPEA'S THE LEADER!
OK, CHICKPEA. WHAT WE NEED IS A PLAN.
A PLAN...
DON'T WORRY...
...I KNOW EXACTLY WHAT TO DO!
PEANUT, I ORDER YOU TO FIGURE OUT HOW TO GET DOWN THE DRAIN TO RESCUE THAT PEA.
OH, WHAT A GOOD PLAN!
SUCH A GREAT LEADER!

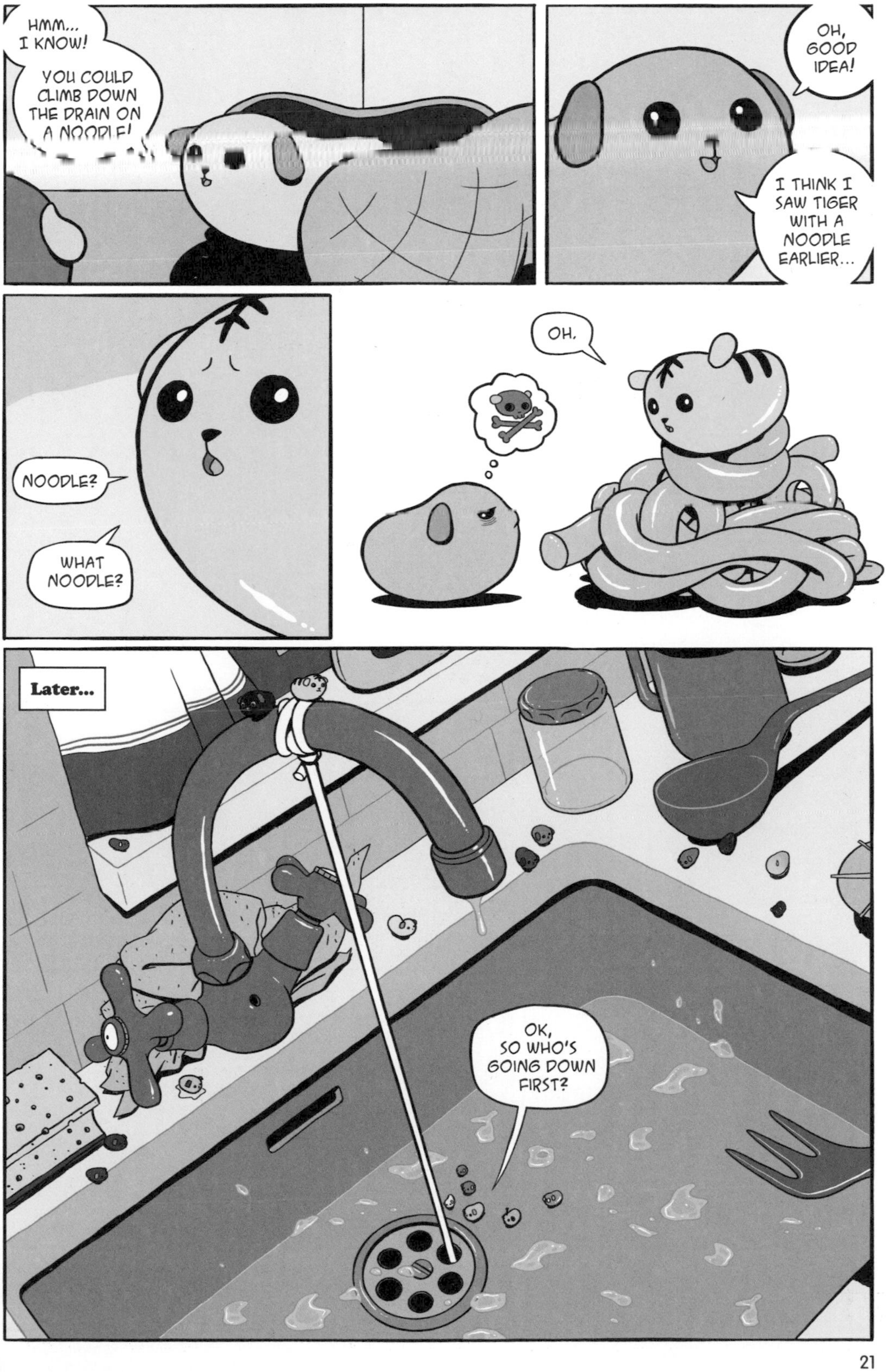

HMM... I KNOW!
YOU COULD CLIMB DOWN THE DRAIN ON A NOODLE!
OH, GOOD IDEA!
I THINK I SAW TIGER WITH A NOODLE EARLIER...
NOODLE?
WHAT NOODLE?
OH.
Later...
OK, SO WHO'S GOING DOWN FIRST?

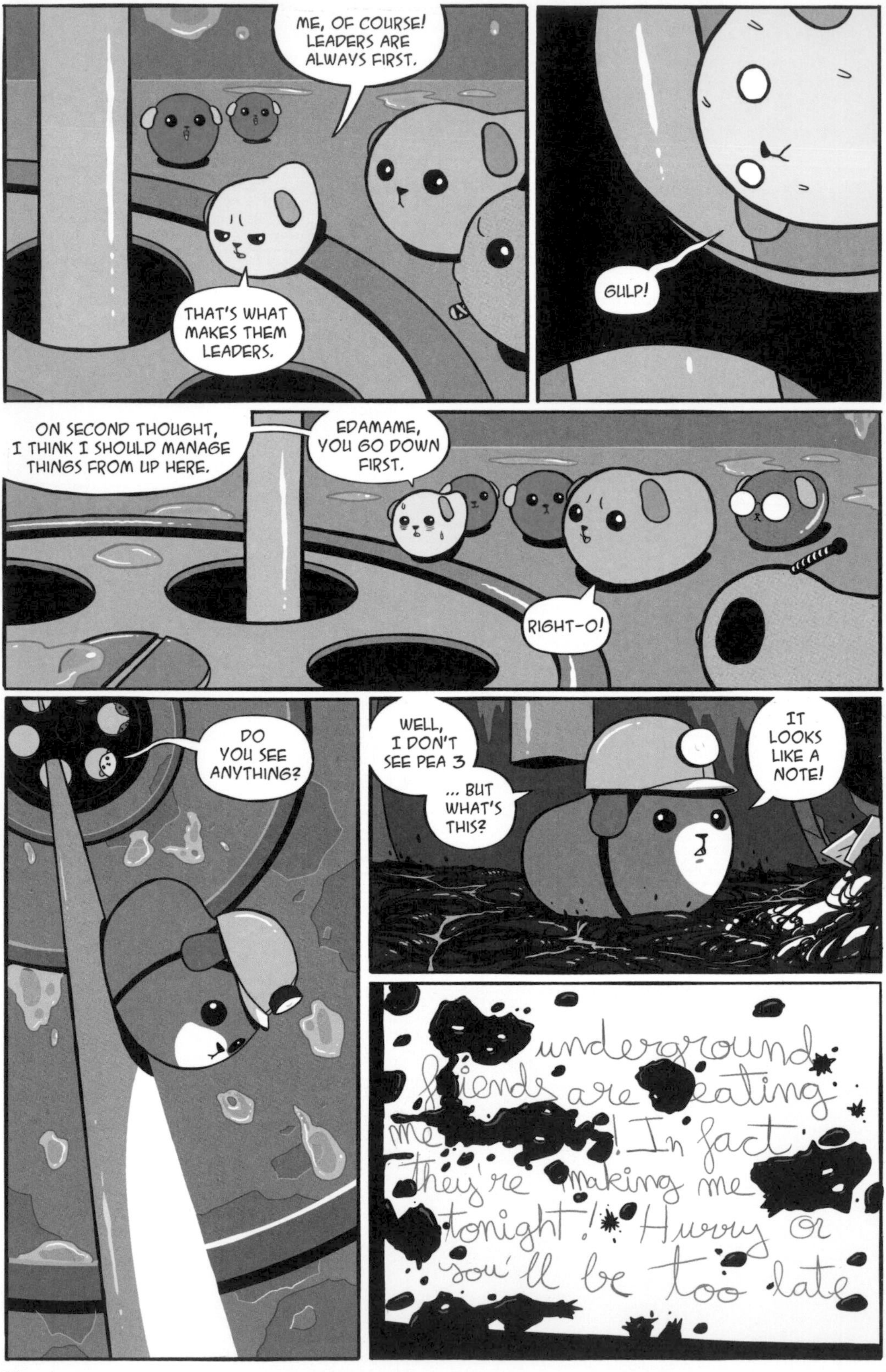
ME, OF COURSE! LEADERS ARE ALWAYS FIRST.
THAT'S WHAT MAKES THEM LEADERS.
GULP!
ON SECOND THOUGHT, I THINK I SHOULD MANAGE THINGS FROM UP HERE.
EDAMAME, YOU GO DOWN FIRST.
RIGHT-O!
DO YOU SEE ANYTHING?
WELL, I DON'T SEE PEA 3
... BUT WHAT'S THIS?
IT LOOKS LIKE A NOTE!
underground friends are eating me! In fact they're making me tonight! Hurry or you'll be too late

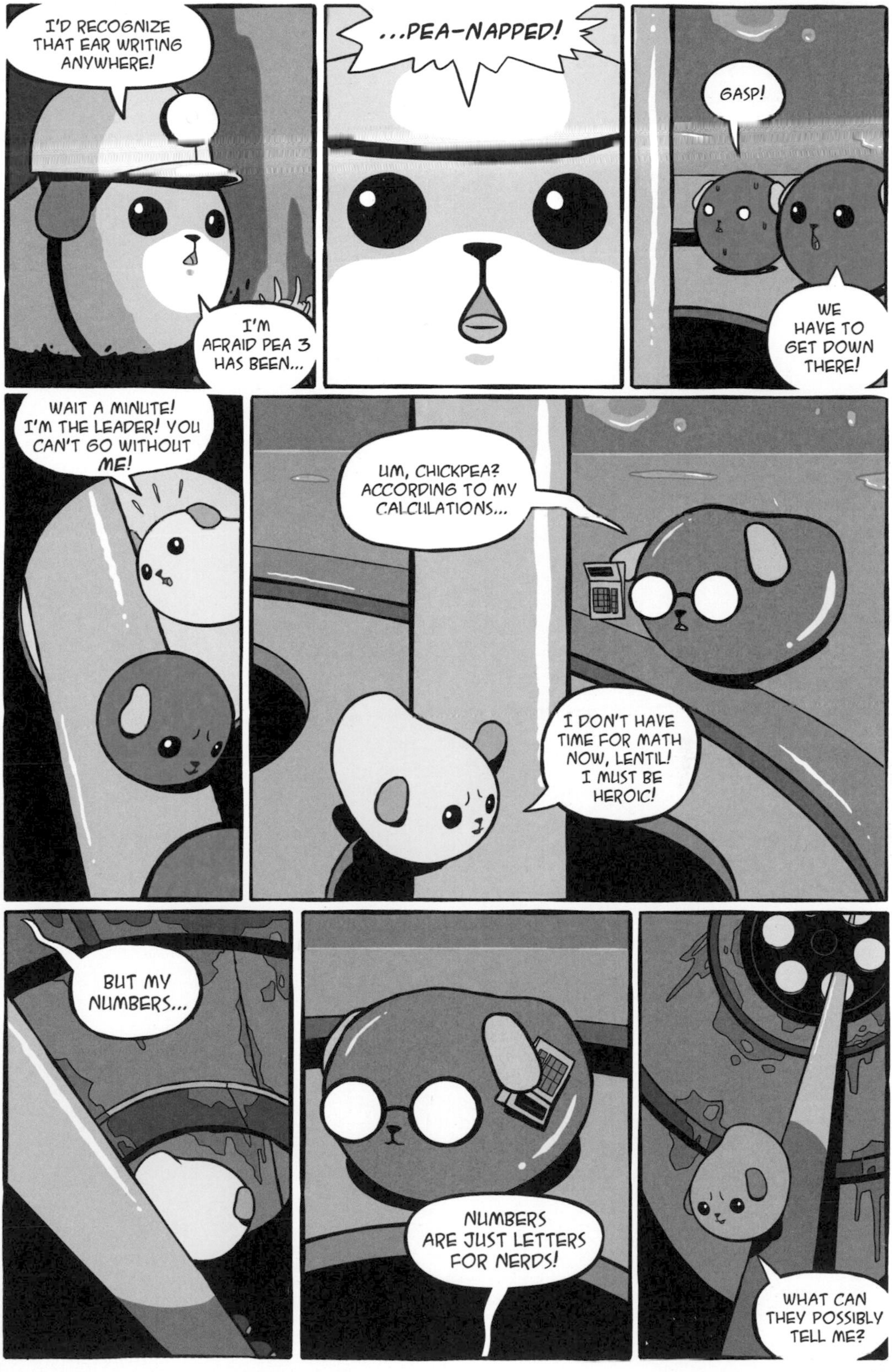
I'D RECOGNIZE THAT EAR WRITING ANYWHERE!
I'M AFRAID PEA 3 HAS BEEN...
...PEA-NAPPED!
GASP!
WE HAVE TO GET DOWN THERE!
WAIT A MINUTE! I'M THE LEADER! YOU CAN'T GO WITHOUT ME!
UM, CHICKPEA? ACCORDING TO MY CALCULATIONS...
I DON'T HAVE TIME FOR MATH NOW, LENTIL! I MUST BE HEROIC!
BUT MY NUMBERS...
NUMBERS ARE JUST LETTERS FOR NERDS!
WHAT CAN THEY POSSIBLY TELL ME?

THAT THIS NOODLE ISN'T STRONG ENOUGH TO HOLD THE WEIGHT OF ALL THREE OF YOU.

OH...

SNAP!

WWOOO!

AAAHH!

WHY DO I SUDDENLY HAVE A BAD FEELING...?

BAM!

OOF!

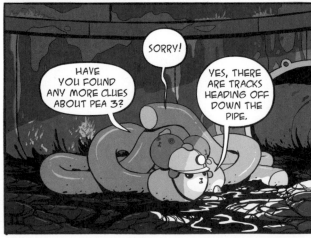

HAVE YOU FOUND ANY MORE CLUES ABOUT PEA 3?

SORRY!

YES, THERE ARE TRACKS HEADING OFF DOWN THE PIPE.

NEVER MIND THAT!

HOW ARE WE GOING TO GET BACK UP?

BRAVE WARRIORS! THE NOBLE NOODLE HAS BEEN TORN ASUNDER BY YOUR EAGERNESS.

...BUT FEAR NOT!

WE SHALL FIND ANOTHER WAY TO RETRIEVE YOU FROM THE TERRIBLE DEPTHS!

BUT WE DON'T HAVE TIME TO WAIT!

WE'VE GOT TO FOLLOW THE TRACKS!

OH NO, I'M STAYING RIGHT HERE AND WAITING FOR THE RESCUE PARTY.

SUIT YOURSELF, CHICKPEA.

COME ON, PEAS!

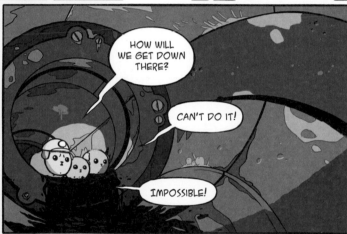

HOW WILL WE GET DOWN THERE?

CAN'T DO IT!

IMPOSSIBLE!

Meanwhile, back in the kitchen

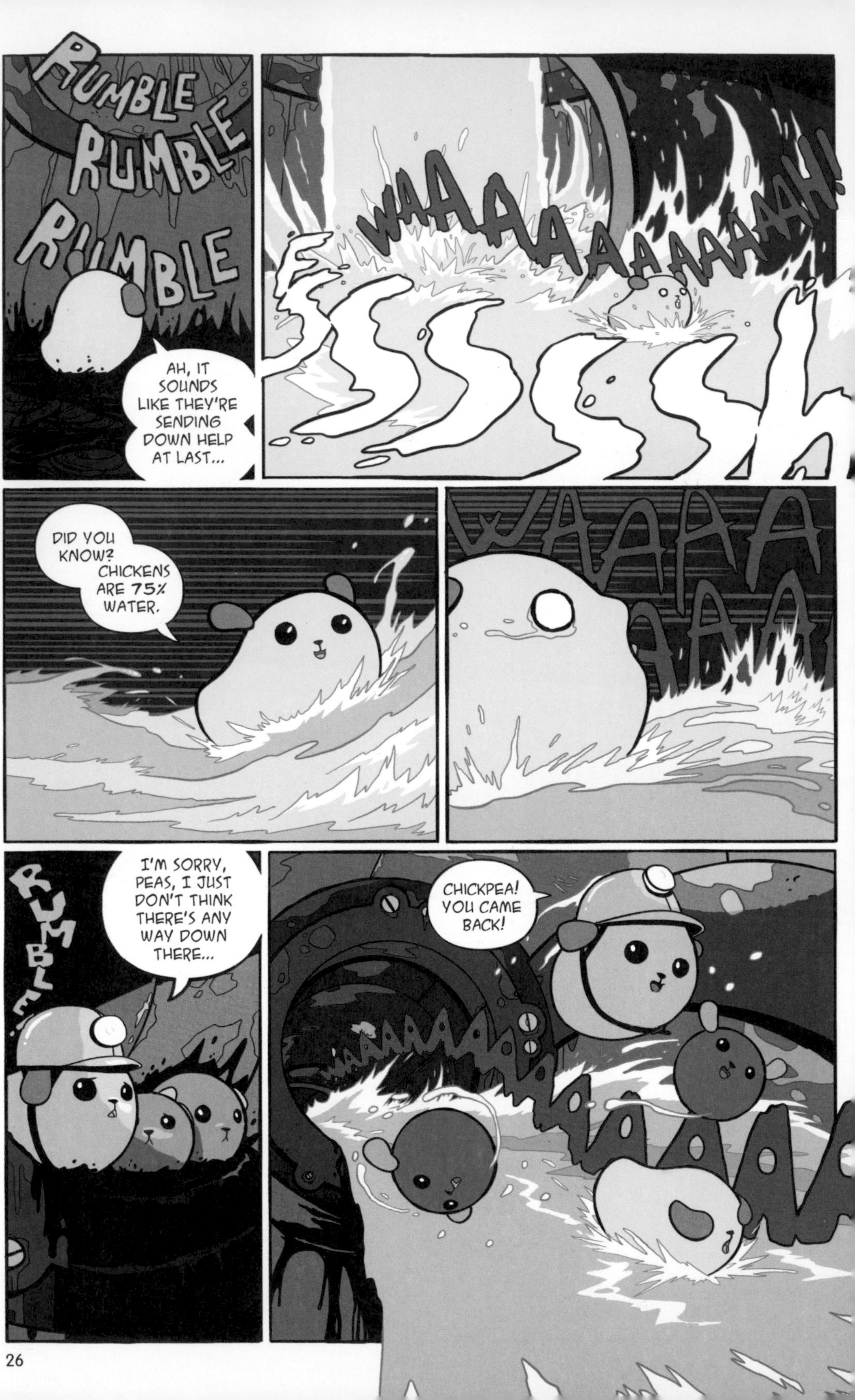
RUMBLE
RUMBLE
RUMBLE
AH, IT SOUNDS LIKE THEY'RE SENDING DOWN HELP AT LAST...
WAAAAAAAAAAAH!
SSSSSH
DID YOU KNOW? CHICKENS ARE 75% WATER.
WAAAAAAA
RUMBLE...
I'M SORRY, PEAS, I JUST DON'T THINK THERE'S ANY WAY DOWN THERE...
CHICKPEA! YOU CAME BACK!
WAAAAAAAAAAA

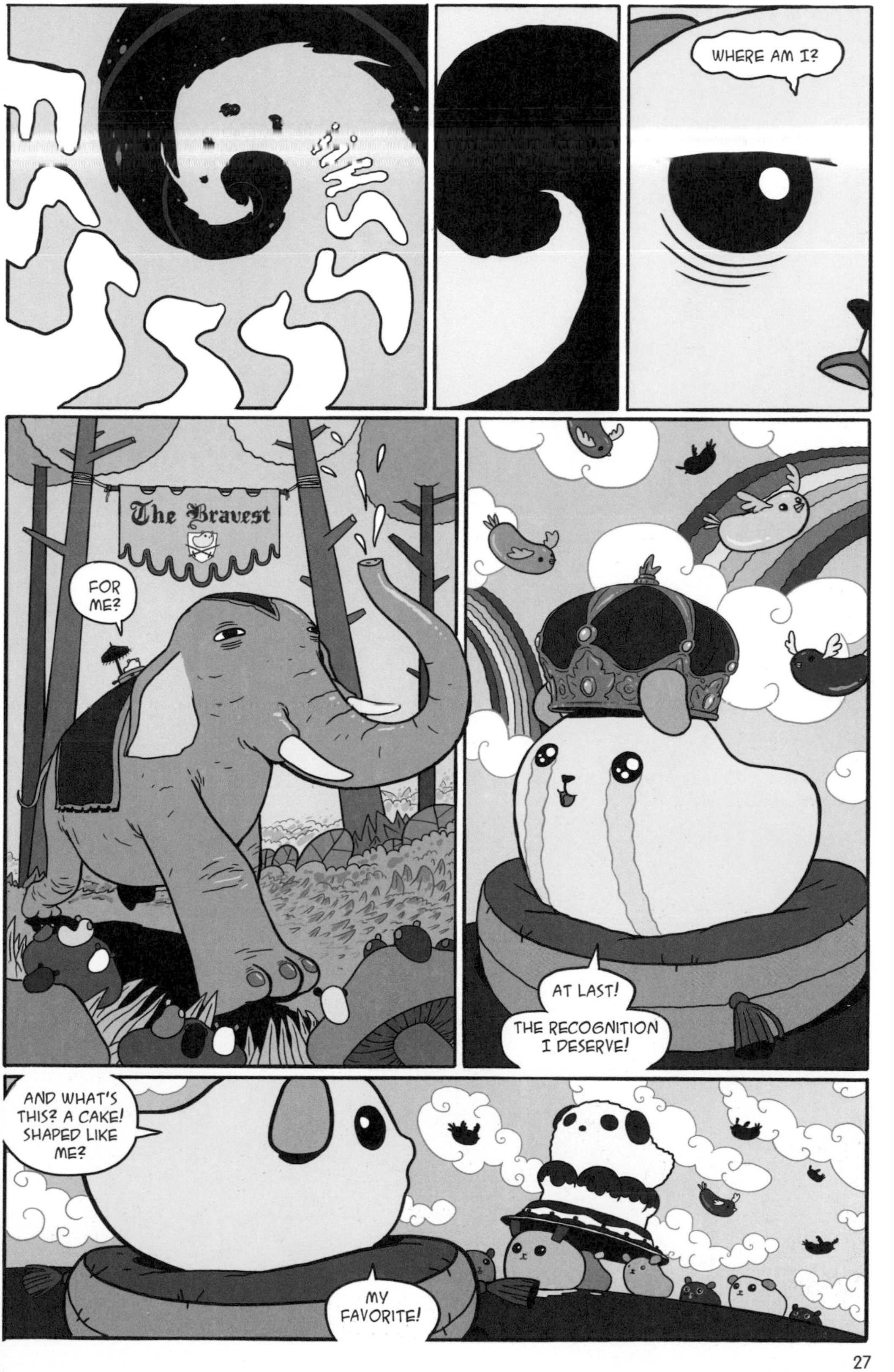
WHERE AM I?
The Bravest
FOR ME?
AT LAST!
THE RECOGNITION I DESERVE!
AND WHAT'S THIS? A CAKE! SHAPED LIKE ME?
MY FAVORITE!

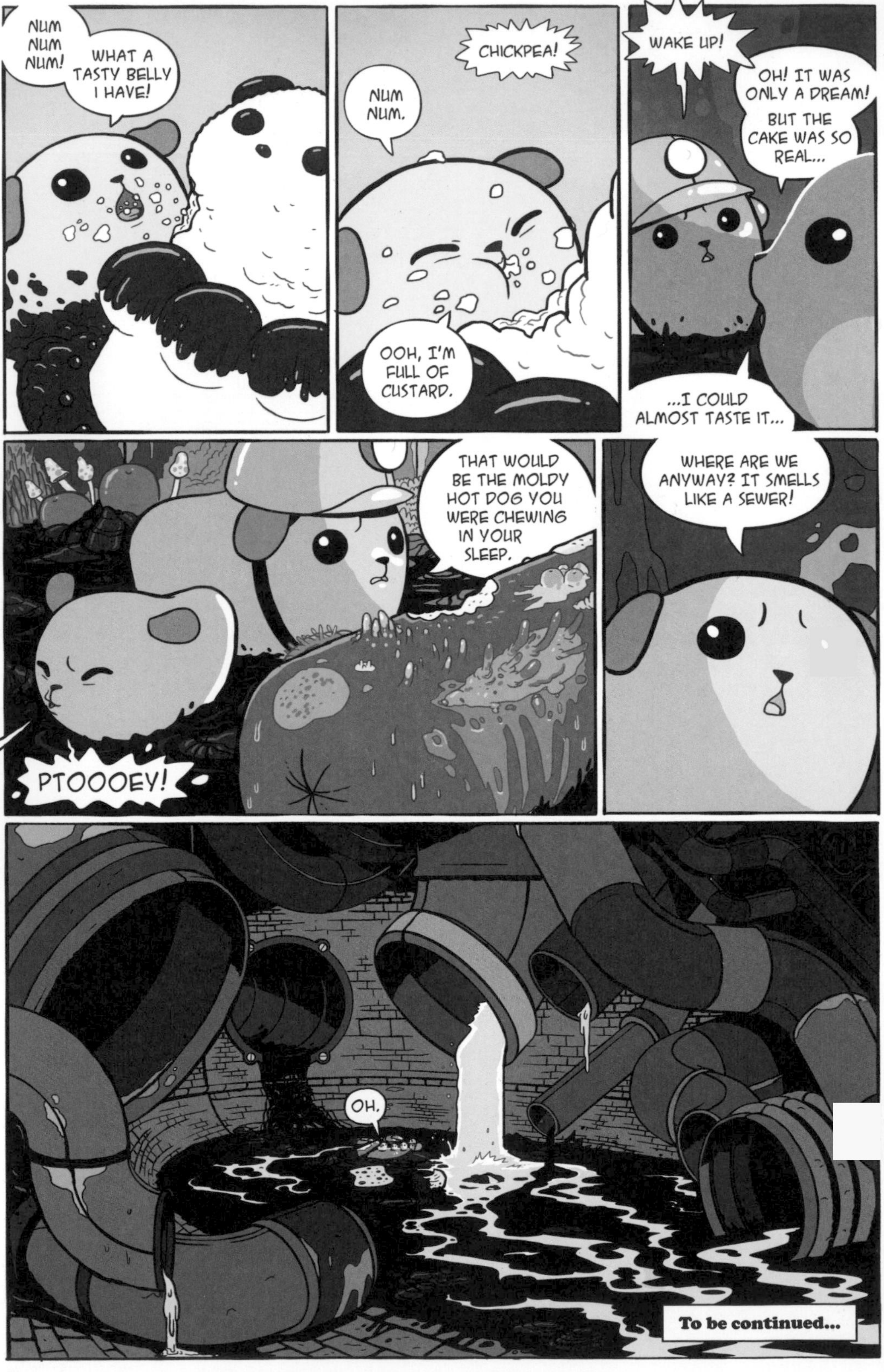
NUM NUM NUM!
WHAT A TASTY BELLY I HAVE!
CHICKPEA!
NUM NUM.
OOH, I'M FULL OF CUSTARD.
WAKE UP!
OH! IT WAS ONLY A DREAM!
BUT THE CAKE WAS SO REAL...
...I COULD ALMOST TASTE IT...
THAT WOULD BE THE MOLDY HOT DOG YOU WERE CHEWING IN YOUR SLEEP.
PTOOOEY!
WHERE ARE WE ANYWAY? IT SMELLS LIKE A SEWER!
OH.
To be continued...

mameshiba

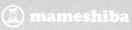

On the LOOSE!

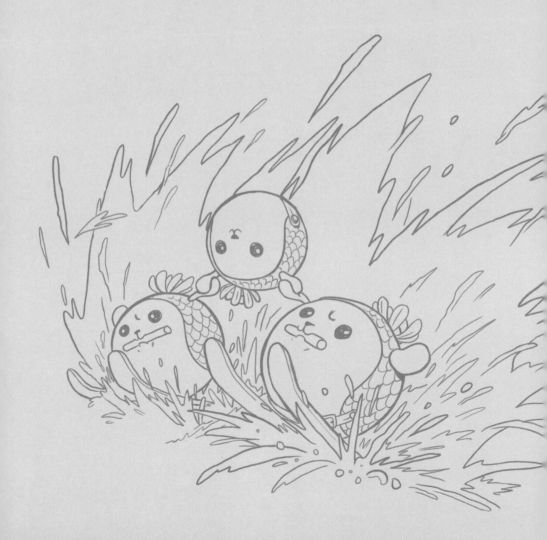

LEARNING JAPANESE WITH THE JELLY BEANS

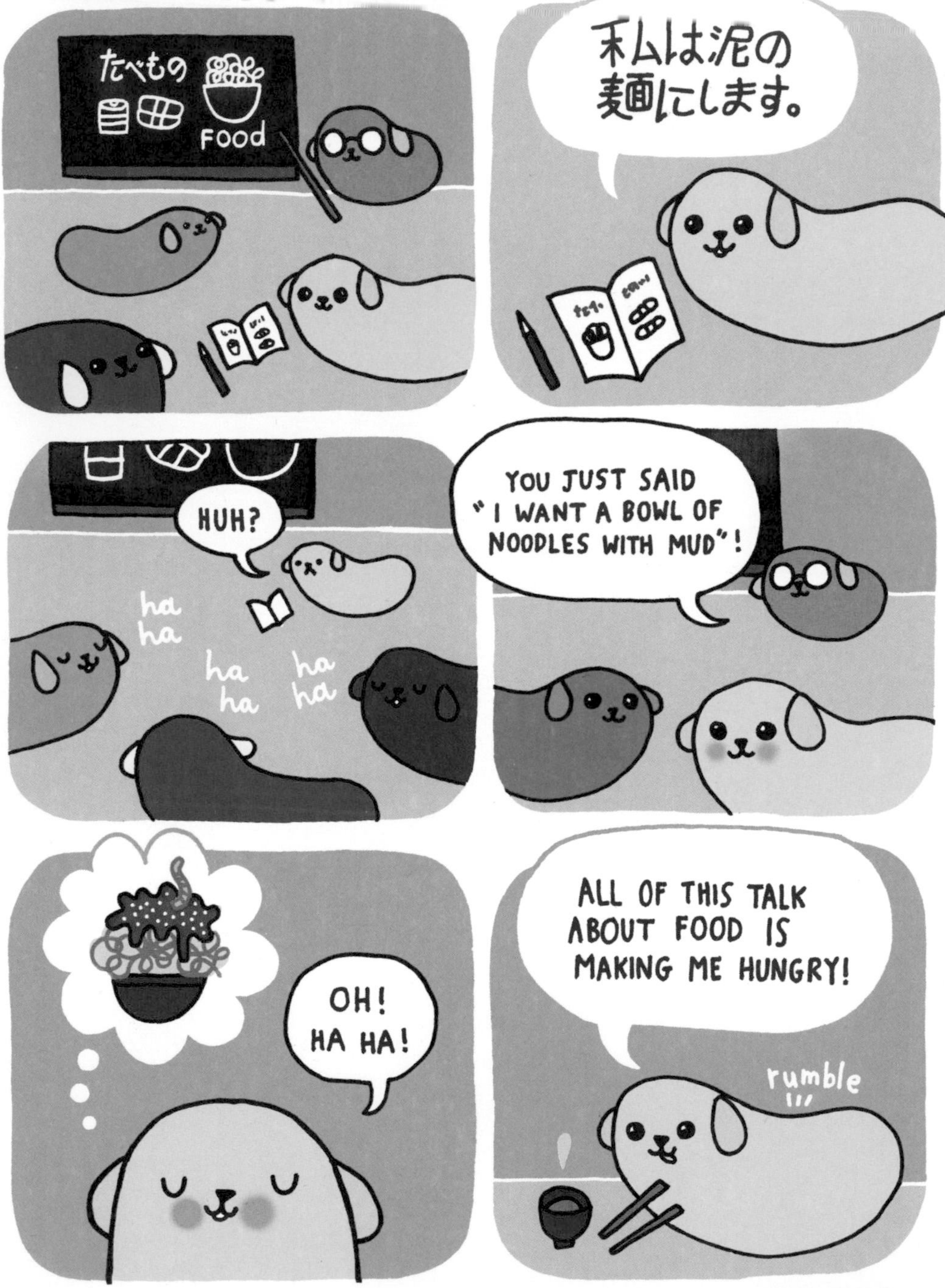

たべもの
Food
私は泥の麺にします。
HUH?
ha ha
ha ha
ha ha
YOU JUST SAID "I WANT A BOWL OF NOODLES WITH MUD"!
OH! HA HA!
ALL OF THIS TALK ABOUT FOOD IS MAKING ME HUNGRY!
rumble

THE END.

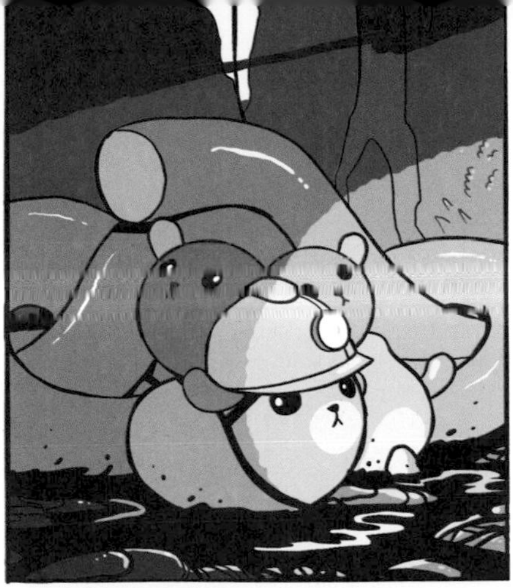

When we last saw our heroes, they were deep in the pipes under the sink, searching for their missing friend. Let's join Edamame, Chickpea and the Green Peas as they continue on their quest in…

Journey to the Center of the Sink Part 2!

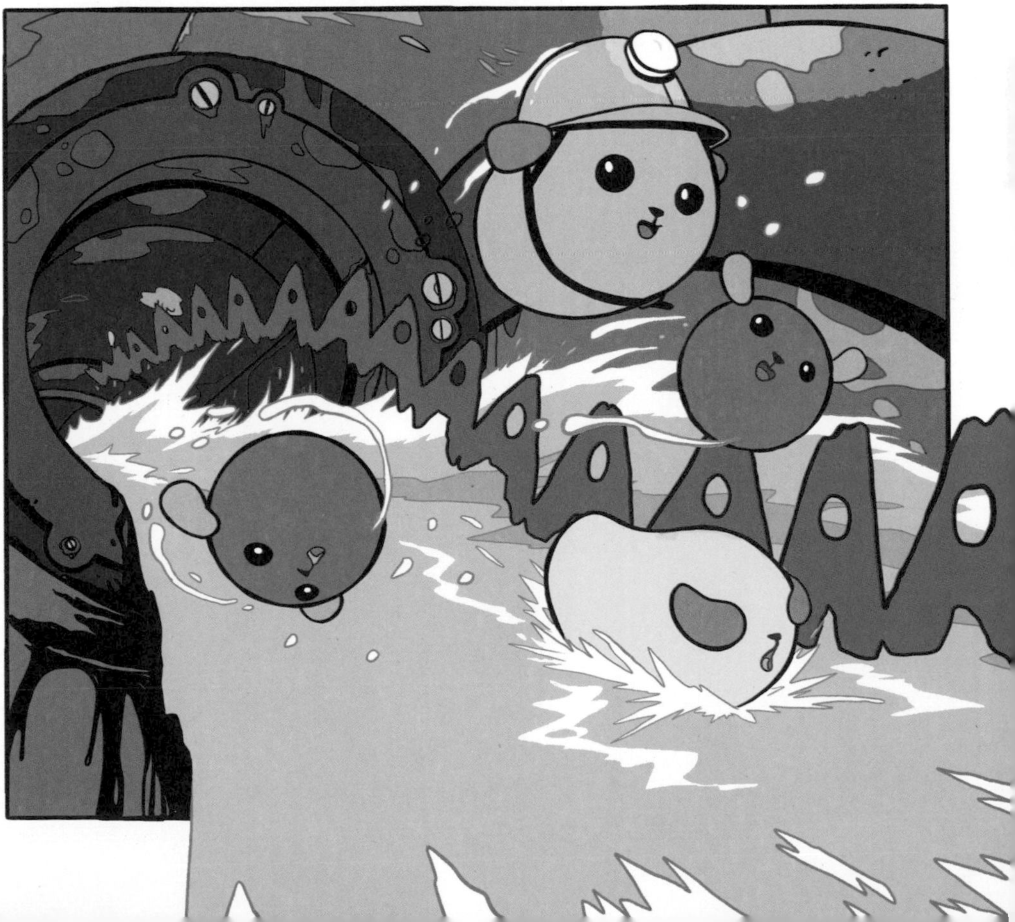

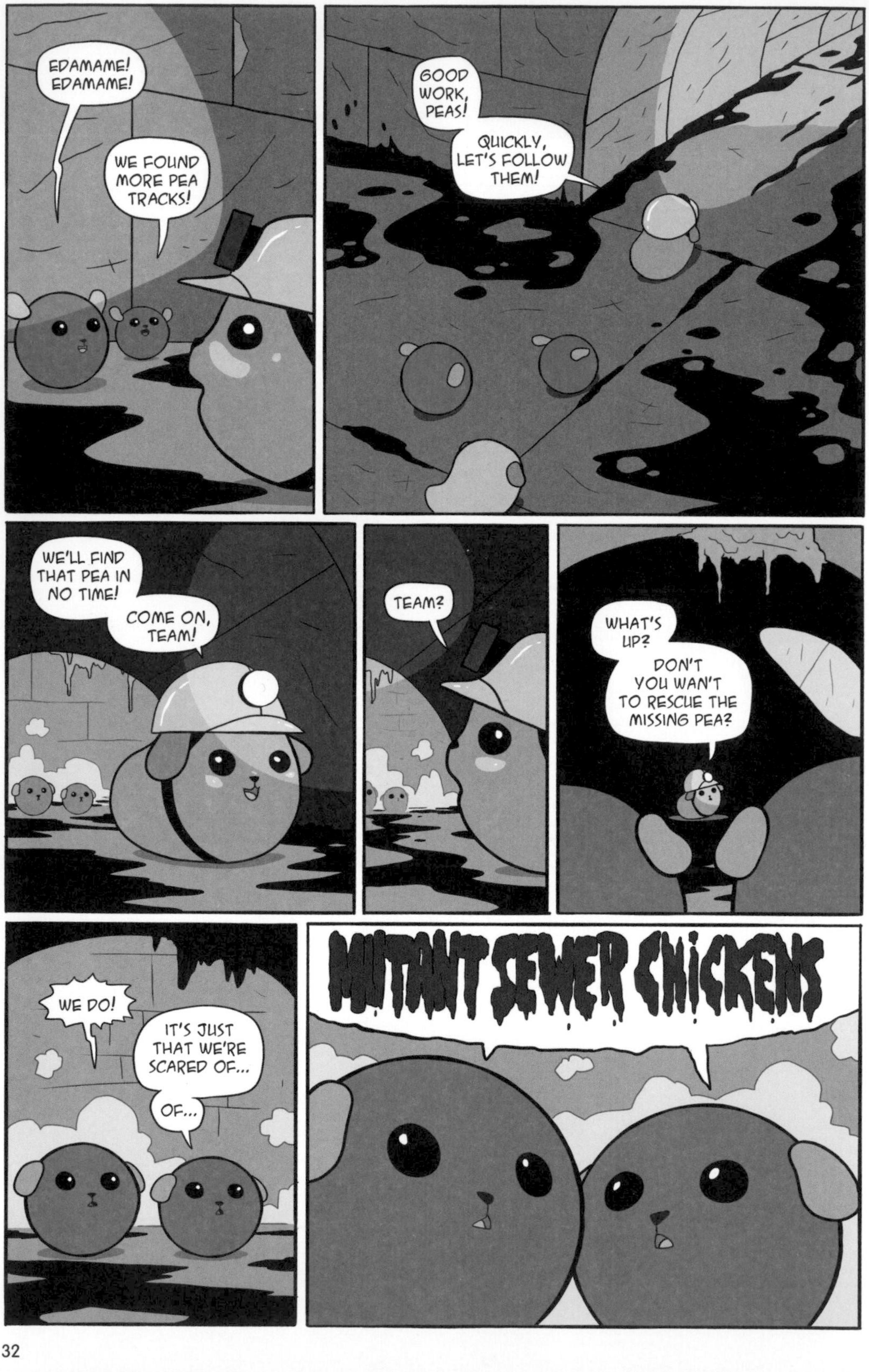
EDAMAME! EDAMAME!
WE FOUND MORE PEA TRACKS!
GOOD WORK, PEAS!
QUICKLY, LET'S FOLLOW THEM!
WE'LL FIND THAT PEA IN NO TIME!
COME ON, TEAM!
TEAM?
WHAT'S UP?
DON'T YOU WAN'T TO RESCUE THE MISSING PEA?
WE DO!
IT'S JUST THAT WE'RE SCARED OF...
OF...
MUTANT SEWER CHICKENS

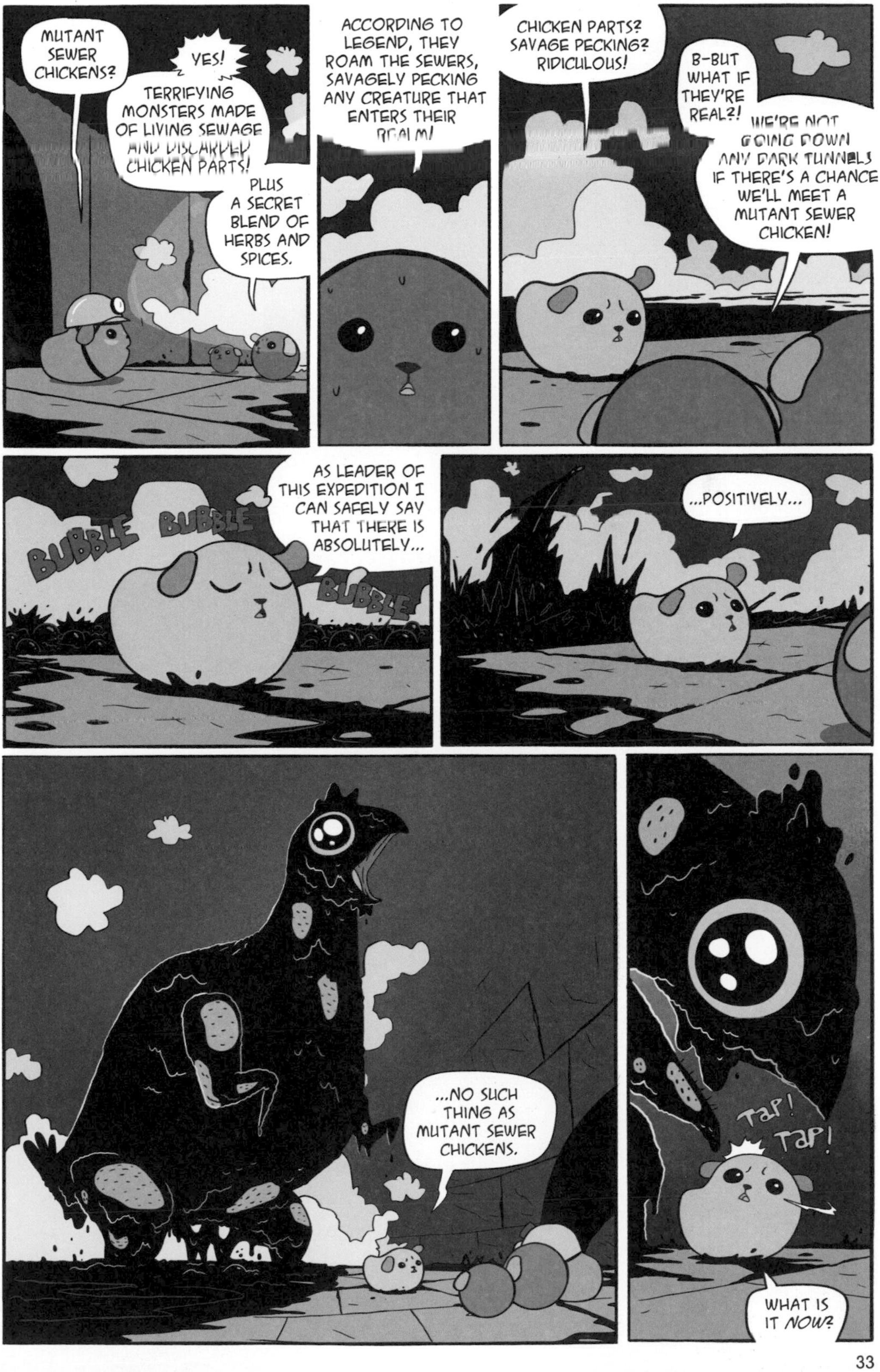
MUTANT SEWER CHICKENS?
YES!
TERRIFYING MONSTERS MADE OF LIVING SEWAGE AND DISCARDED CHICKEN PARTS!
PLUS A SECRET BLEND OF HERBS AND SPICES.
ACCORDING TO LEGEND, THEY ROAM THE SEWERS, SAVAGELY PECKING ANY CREATURE THAT ENTERS THEIR REALM!
CHICKEN PARTS? SAVAGE PECKING? RIDICULOUS!
B-BUT WHAT IF THEY'RE REAL?!
WE'RE NOT GOING DOWN ANY DARK TUNNELS IF THERE'S A CHANCE WE'LL MEET A MUTANT SEWER CHICKEN!
BUBBLE
BUBBLE
AS LEADER OF THIS EXPEDITION I CAN SAFELY SAY THAT THERE IS ABSOLUTELY...
BUBBLE
...POSITIVELY...
...NO SUCH THING AS MUTANT SEWER CHICKENS.
TAP!
TAP!
WHAT IS IT *NOW*?

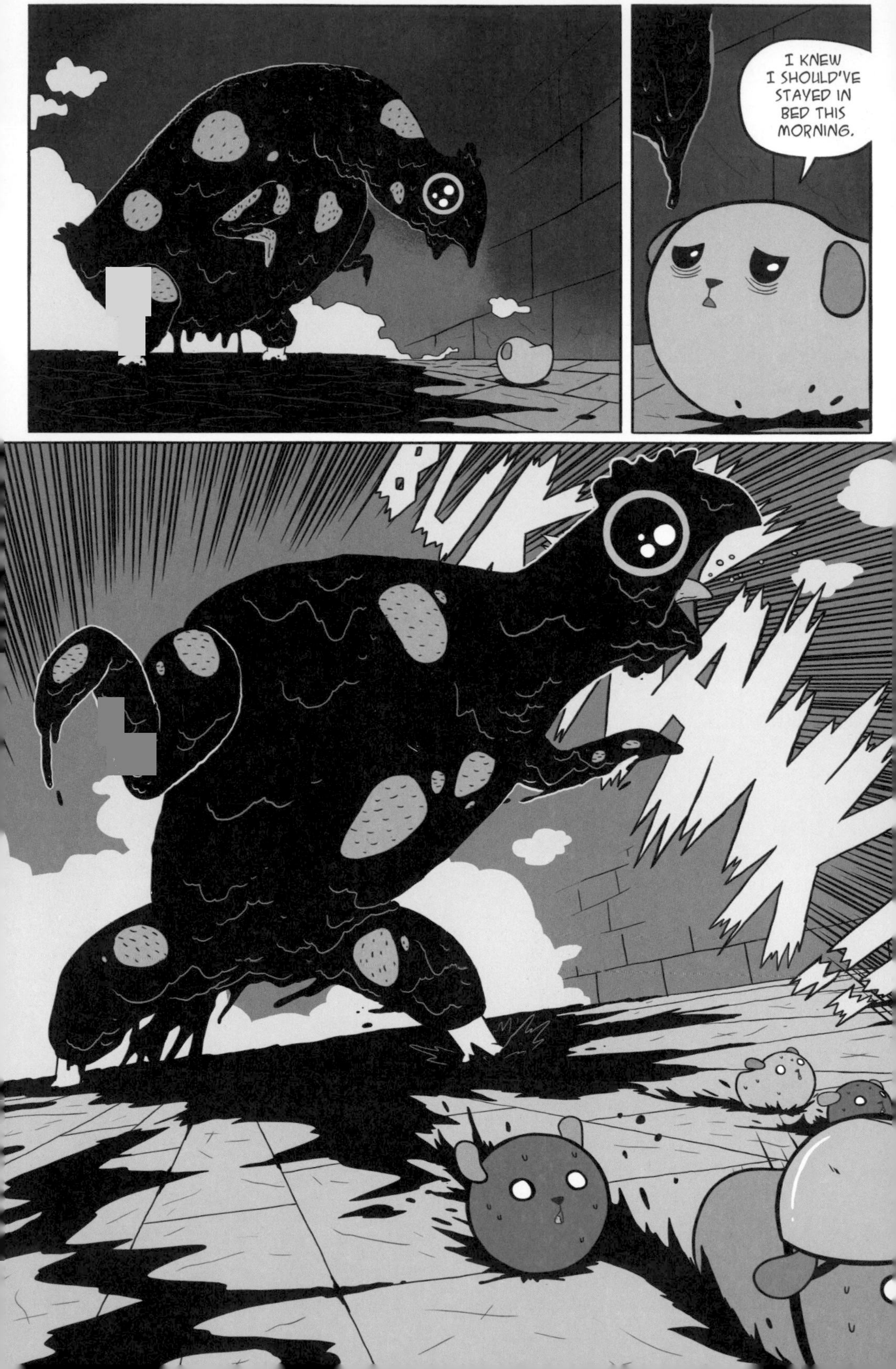
I KNEW I SHOULD'VE STAYED IN BED THIS MORNING.

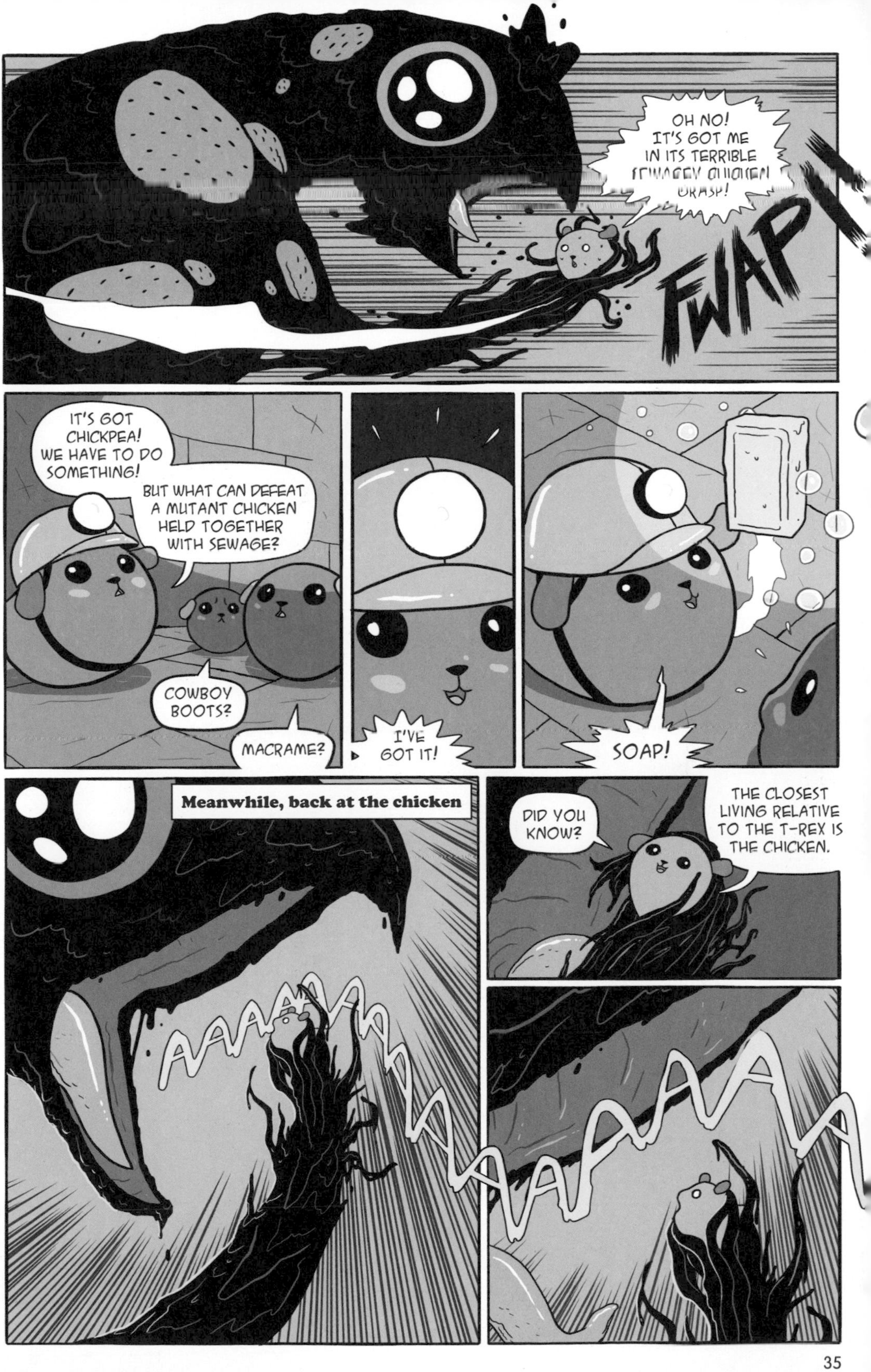

OH NO! IT'S GOT ME IN ITS TERRIBLE SEWAGEY CHICKEN GRASP!
FWAP!!
IT'S GOT CHICKPEA! WE HAVE TO DO SOMETHING!
BUT WHAT CAN DEFEAT A MUTANT CHICKEN HELD TOGETHER WITH SEWAGE?
COWBOY BOOTS?
MACRAME?
I'VE GOT IT!
SOAP!
Meanwhile, back at the chicken
DID YOU KNOW?
THE CLOSEST LIVING RELATIVE TO THE T-REX IS THE CHICKEN.
AAAAAAAAAAAAAAAAAAAA

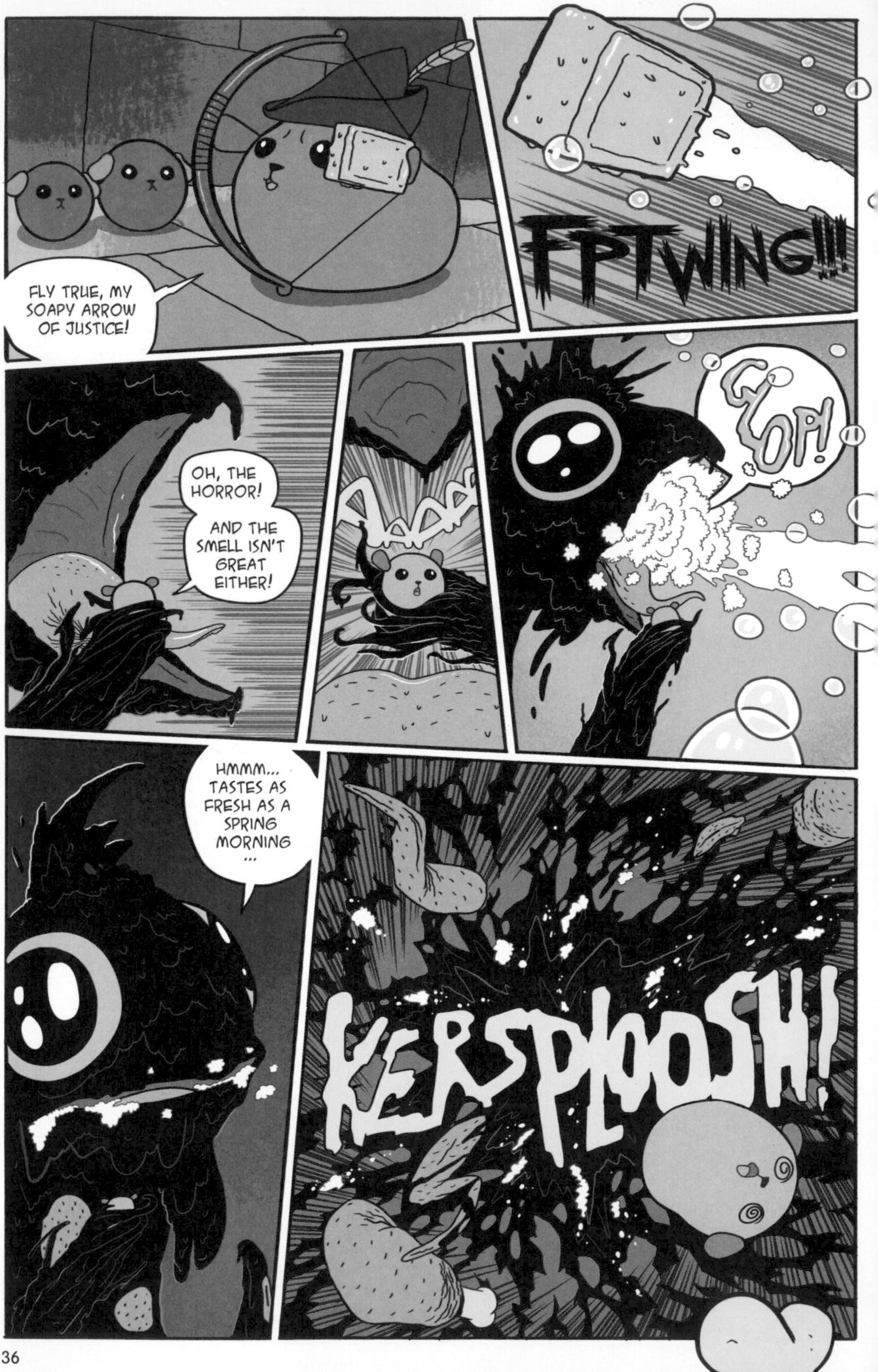
FLY TRUE, MY SOAPY ARROW OF JUSTICE!
FPTWING!!!
OH, THE HORROR!
AND THE SMELL ISN'T GREAT EITHER!
GLOP!
HMMM... TASTES AS FRESH AS A SPRING MORNING ...
KERSPLOOSH!

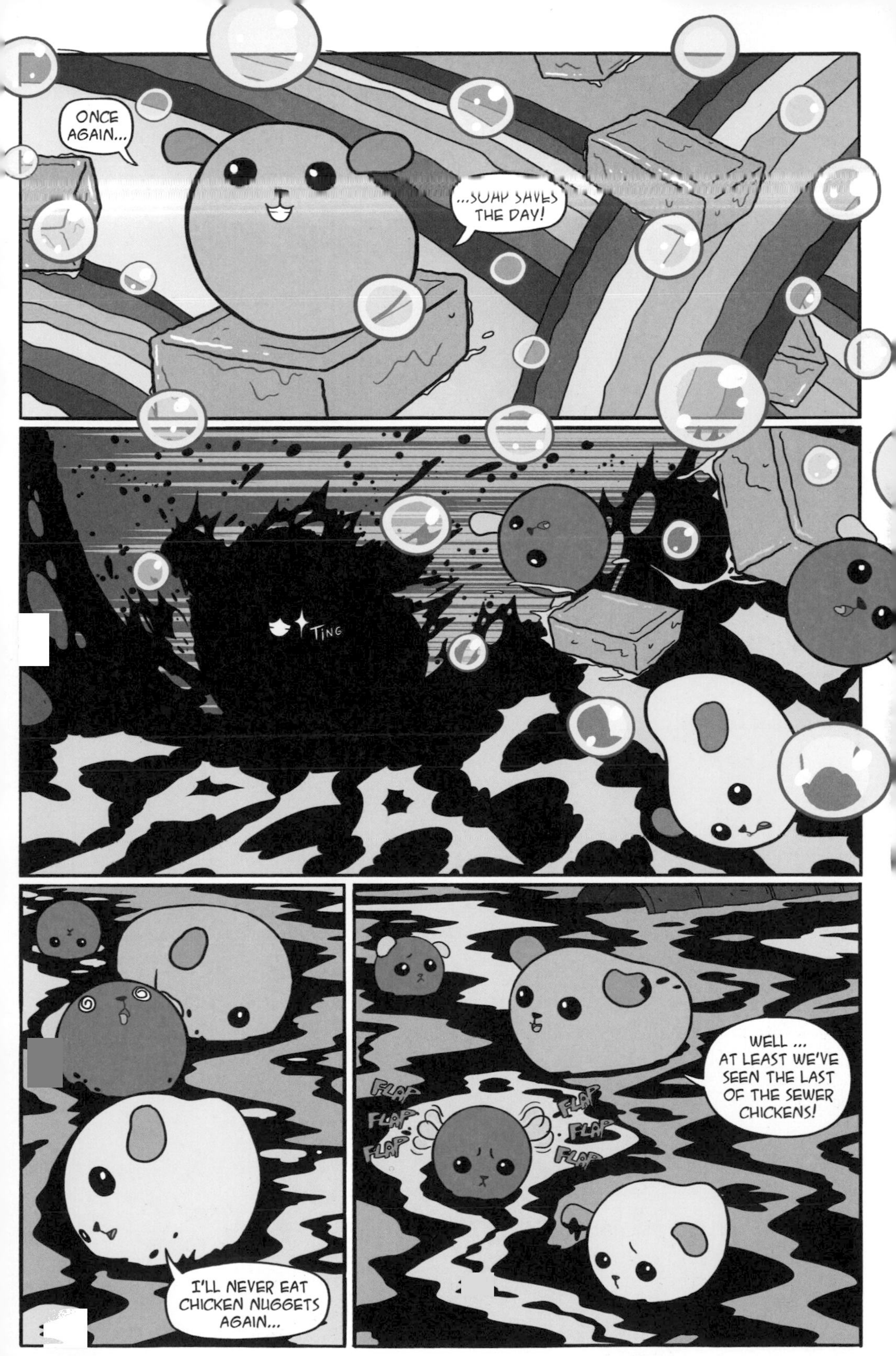

ONCE AGAIN...
...SOAP SAVES THE DAY!
TING
I'LL NEVER EAT CHICKEN NUGGETS AGAIN...
FLAP FLAP FLAP
FLAP FLAP FLAP
WELL ... AT LEAST WE'VE SEEN THE LAST OF THE SEWER CHICKENS!

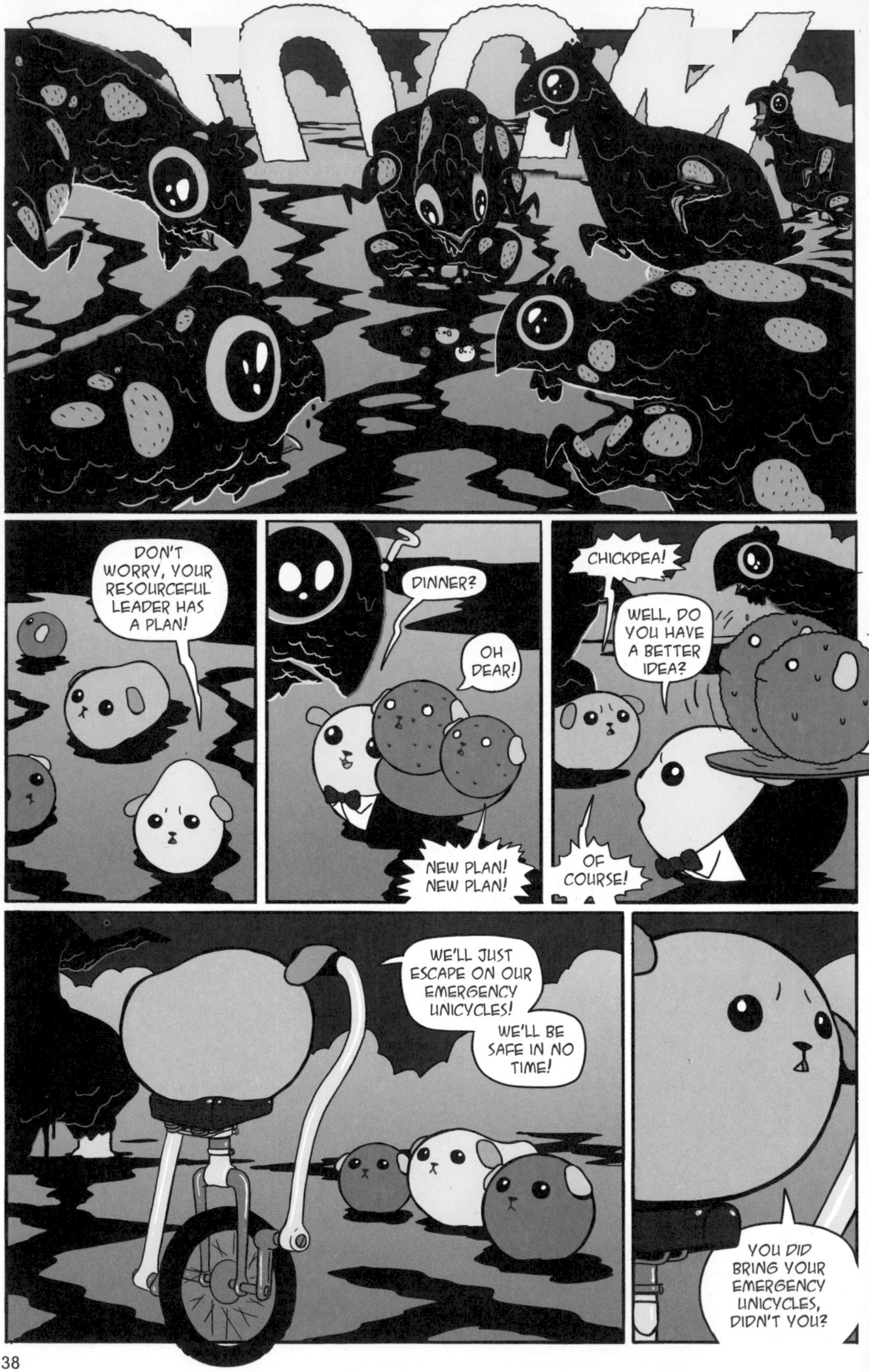
DON'T WORRY, YOUR RESOURCEFUL LEADER HAS A PLAN!
DINNER?
OH DEAR!
NEW PLAN! NEW PLAN!
CHICKPEA!
WELL, DO YOU HAVE A BETTER IDEA?
OF COURSE!
WE'LL JUST ESCAPE ON OUR EMERGENCY UNICYCLES!
WE'LL BE SAFE IN NO TIME!
YOU DID BRING YOUR EMERGENCY UNICYCLES, DIDN'T YOU?

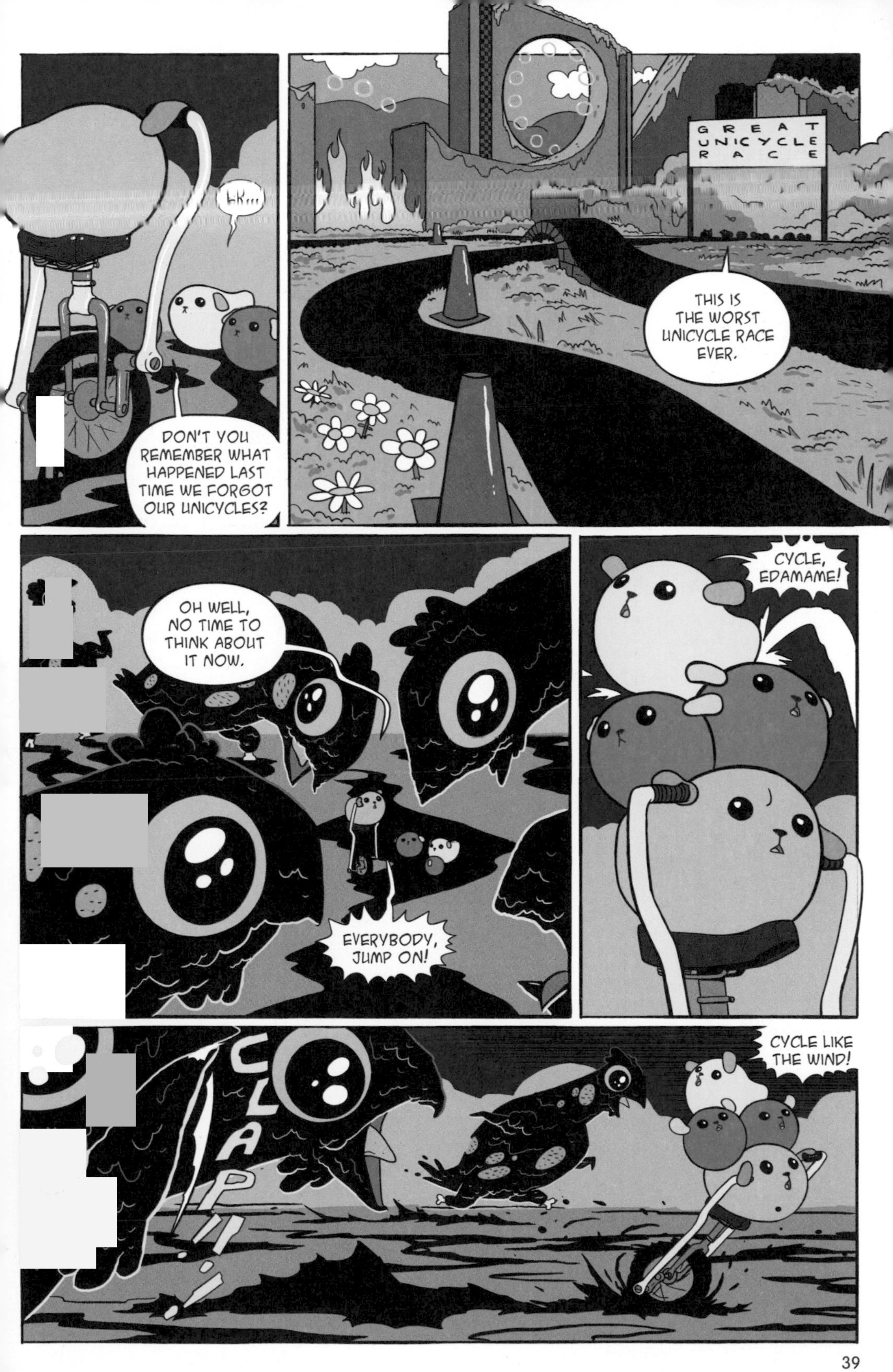
HK...
DON'T YOU REMEMBER WHAT HAPPENED LAST TIME WE FORGOT OUR UNICYCLES?
GREAT UNICYCLE RACE
THIS IS THE WORST UNICYCLE RACE EVER.
OH WELL, NO TIME TO THINK ABOUT IT NOW.
EVERYBODY, JUMP ON!
CYCLE, EDAMAME!
CLAP
CYCLE LIKE THE WIND!

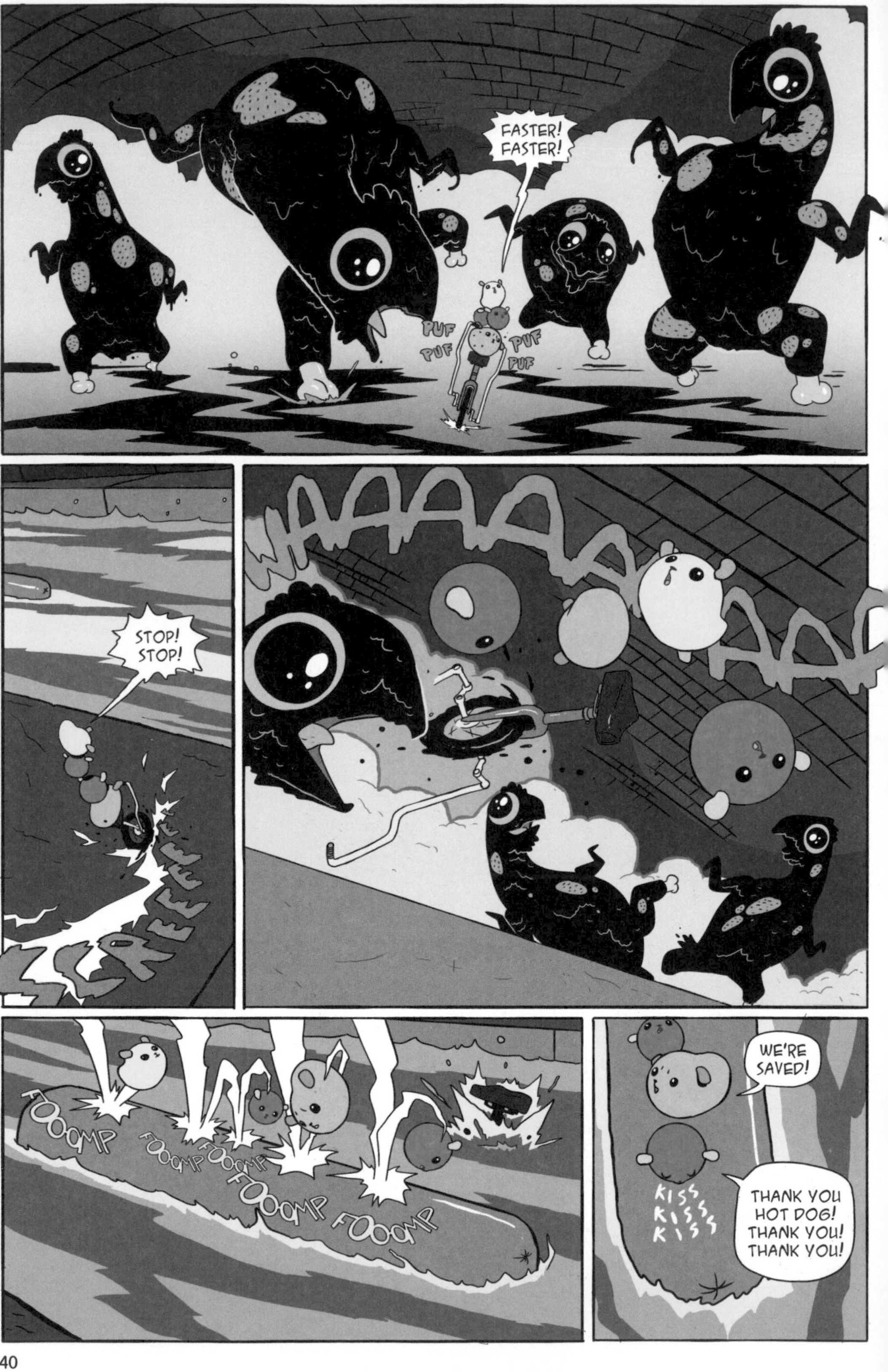
FASTER! FASTER!
PUF PUF PUF PUF
STOP! STOP!
SCREEE
WAAAAAAAA
FOOOMP FOOOMP FOOOMP FOOOMP FOOOMP
WE'RE SAVED!
KISS KISS KISS
THANK YOU HOT DOG! THANK YOU! THANK YOU!

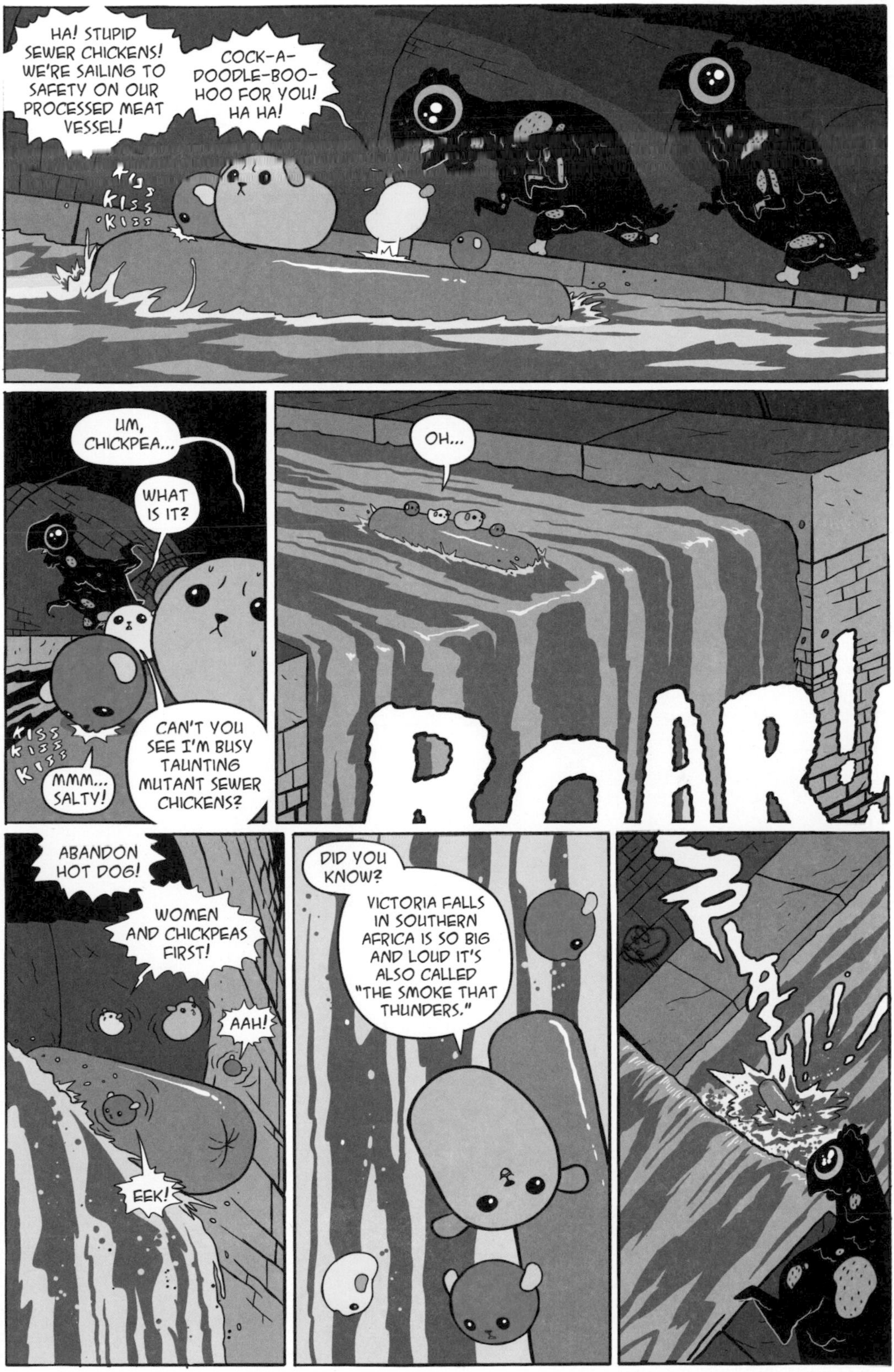
HA! STUPID SEWER CHICKENS! WE'RE SAILING TO SAFETY ON OUR PROCESSED MEAT VESSEL!
COCK-A-DOODLE-BOO-HOO FOR YOU! HA HA!
KISS KISS KISS
UM, CHICKPEA...
WHAT IS IT?
KISS KISS KISS
MMM... SALTY!
CAN'T YOU SEE I'M BUSY TAUNTING MUTANT SEWER CHICKENS?
OH...
ROAR!
ABANDON HOT DOG!
WOMEN AND CHICKPEAS FIRST!
AAH!
EEK!
DID YOU KNOW?
VICTORIA FALLS IN SOUTHERN AFRICA IS SO BIG AND LOUD IT'S ALSO CALLED "THE SMOKE THAT THUNDERS."

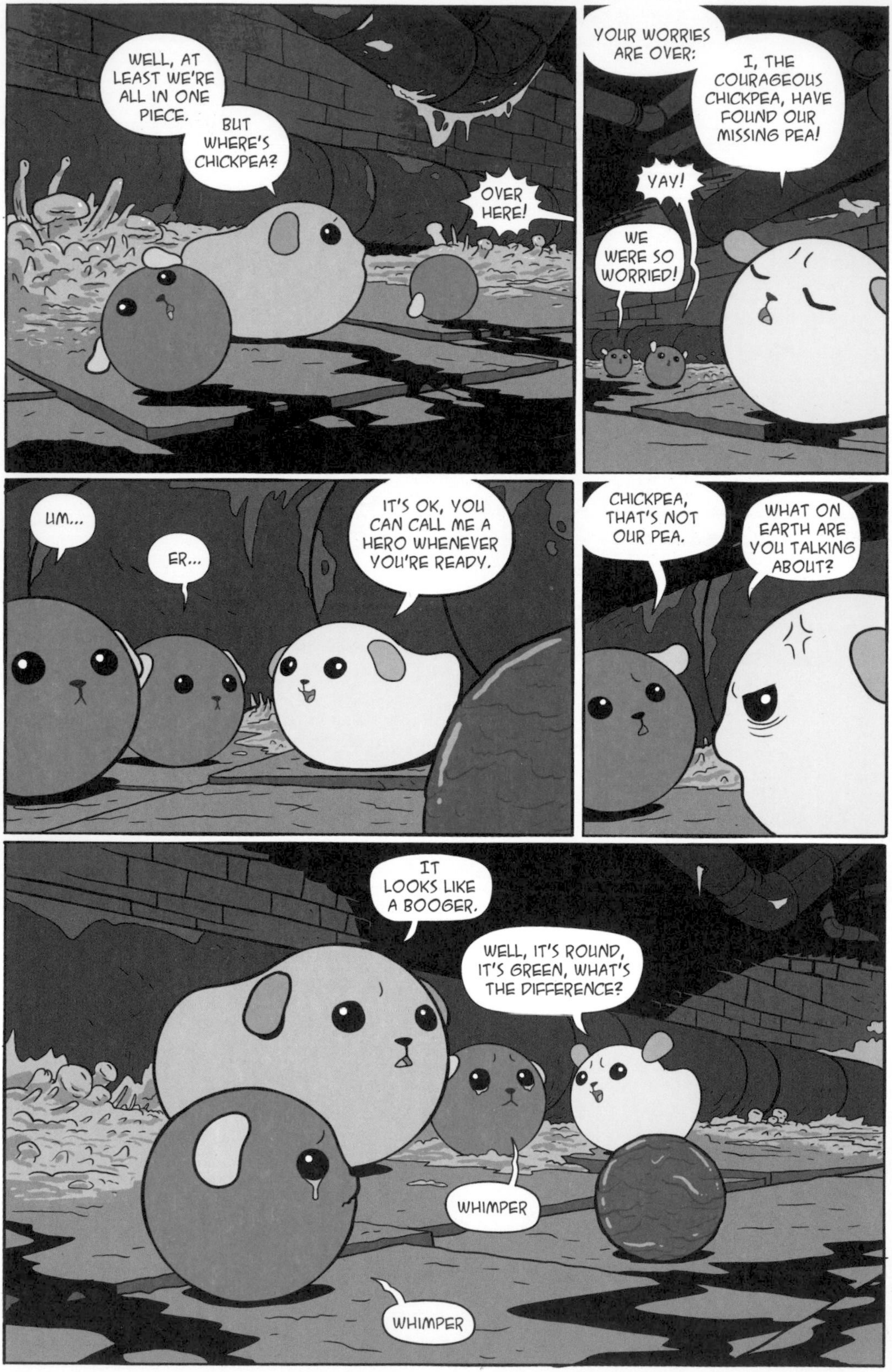
WELL, AT LEAST WE'RE ALL IN ONE PIECE.
BUT WHERE'S CHICKPEA?
OVER HERE!
YOUR WORRIES ARE OVER:
I, THE COURAGEOUS CHICKPEA, HAVE FOUND OUR MISSING PEA!
YAY!
WE WERE SO WORRIED!
UM...
ER...
IT'S OK, YOU CAN CALL ME A HERO WHENEVER YOU'RE READY.
CHICKPEA, THAT'S NOT OUR PEA.
WHAT ON EARTH ARE YOU TALKING ABOUT?
IT LOOKS LIKE A BOOGER.
WELL, IT'S ROUND, IT'S GREEN, WHAT'S THE DIFFERENCE?
WHIMPER
WHIMPER

WAAAAAAAA

BAH! I DON'T KNOW WHY I EVEN BOTHER IF THIS IS THE THANKS I GET!

SNIFF! SNIFF!

DO YOU SMELL THAT?

W-WHAT DO YOU SMELL, EDAMAME?

I SMELL...

PEA!

WELL WE ARE IN A SEWER...

NO, NO! I MEAN PEA 3!

OH YES, I SMELL IT TOO!

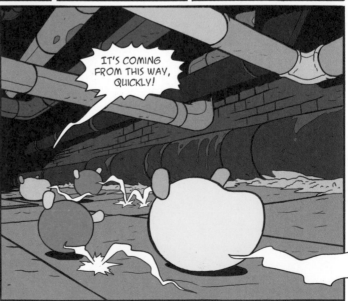

IT'S COMING FROM THIS WAY, QUICKLY!

43

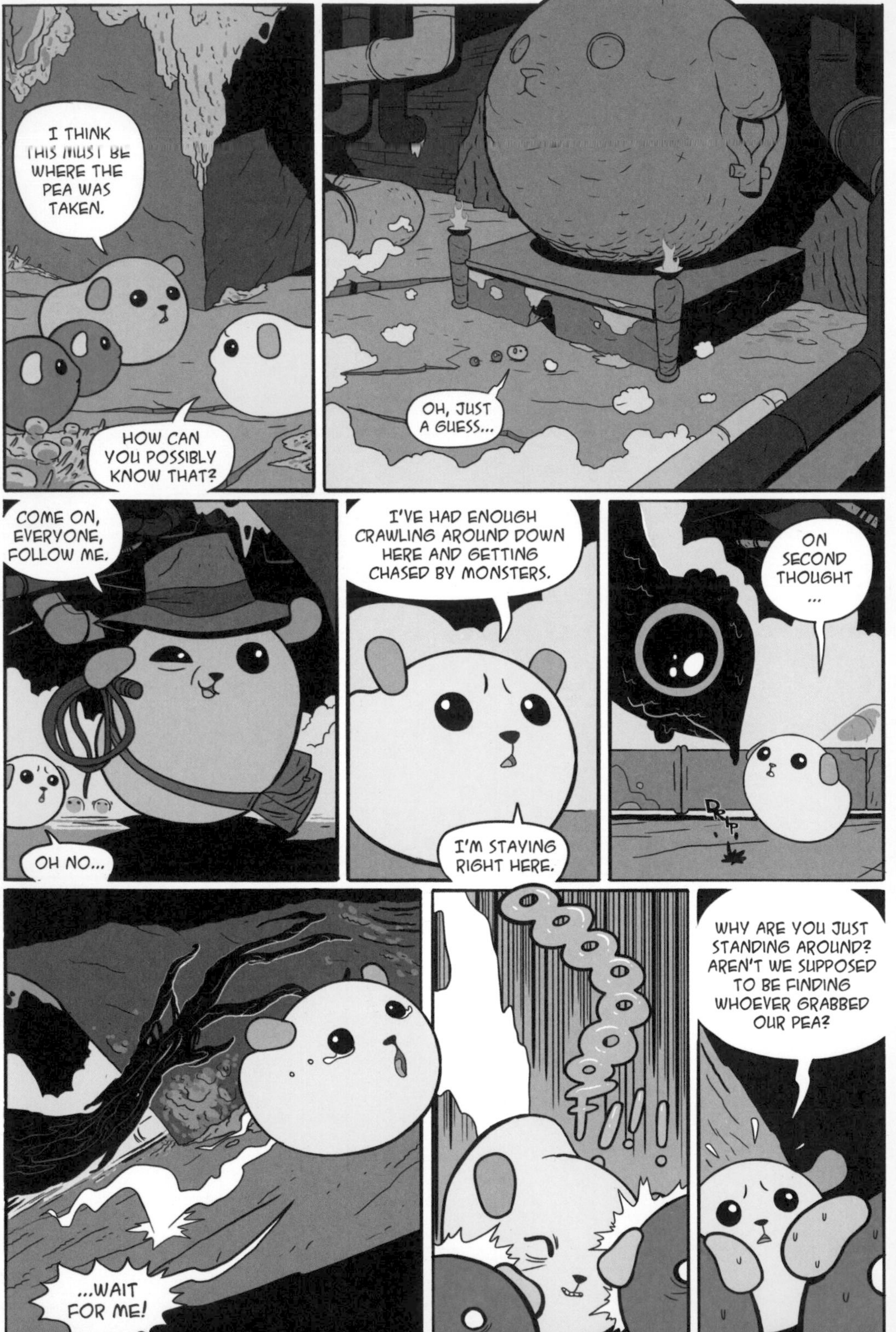
I THINK THIS MUST BE WHERE THE PEA WAS TAKEN.
HOW CAN YOU POSSIBLY KNOW THAT?
OH, JUST A GUESS...
COME ON, EVERYONE, FOLLOW ME.
OH NO...
I'VE HAD ENOUGH CRAWLING AROUND DOWN HERE AND GETTING CHASED BY MONSTERS.
I'M STAYING RIGHT HERE.
ON SECOND THOUGHT ...
DRIP
...WAIT FOR ME!
WHY ARE YOU JUST STANDING AROUND? AREN'T WE SUPPOSED TO BE FINDING WHOEVER GRABBED OUR PEA?

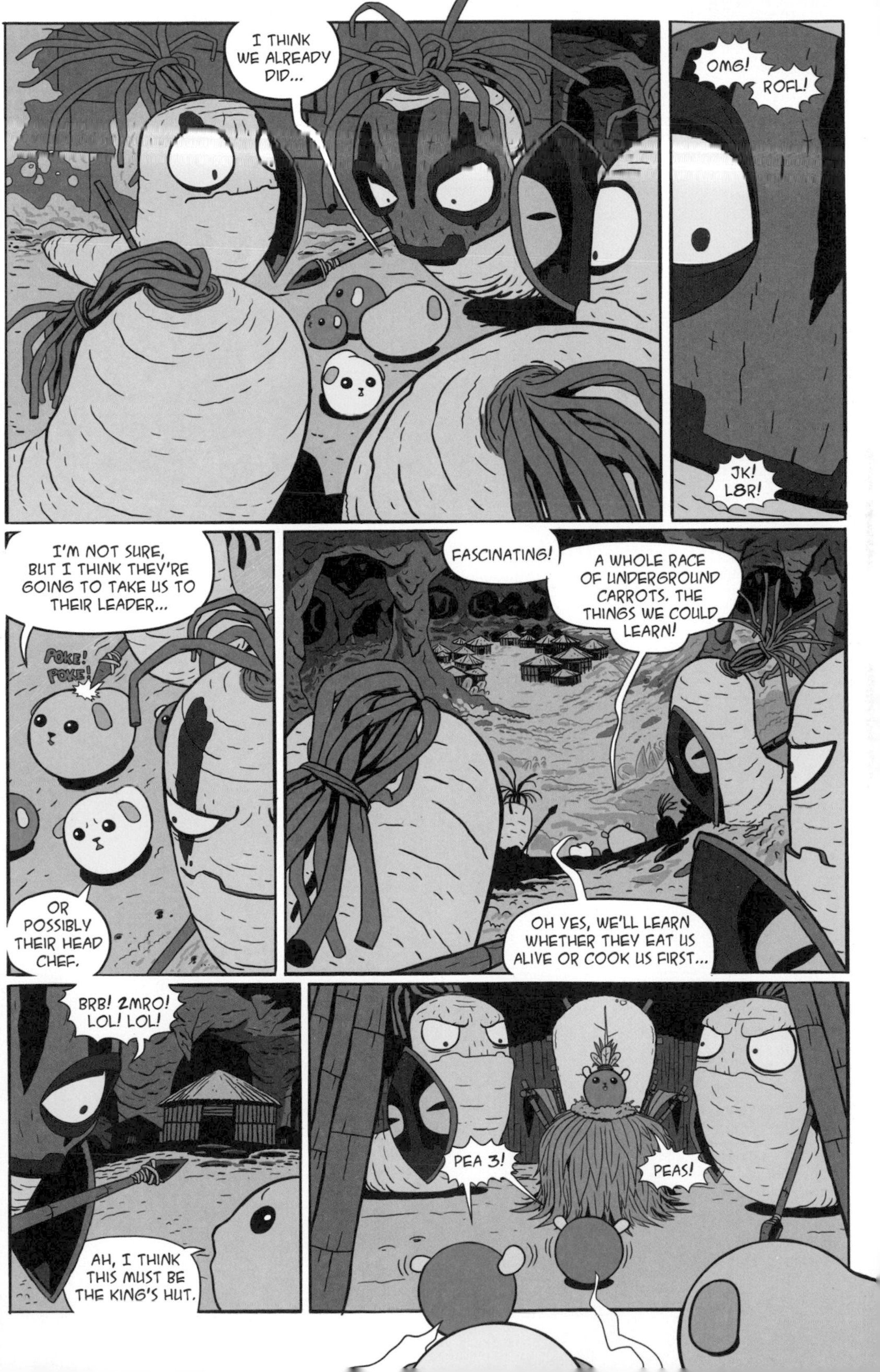
I THINK WE ALREADY DID...
OMG!
ROFL!
JK! L8R!
I'M NOT SURE, BUT I THINK THEY'RE GOING TO TAKE US TO THEIR LEADER...
POKE! POKE!
OR POSSIBLY THEIR HEAD CHEF.
FASCINATING!
A WHOLE RACE OF UNDERGROUND CARROTS. THE THINGS WE COULD LEARN!
OH YES, WE'LL LEARN WHETHER THEY EAT US ALIVE OR COOK US FIRST...
BRB! 2MRO! LOL! LOL!
AH, I THINK THIS MUST BE THE KING'S HUT.
PEA 3!
PEAS!

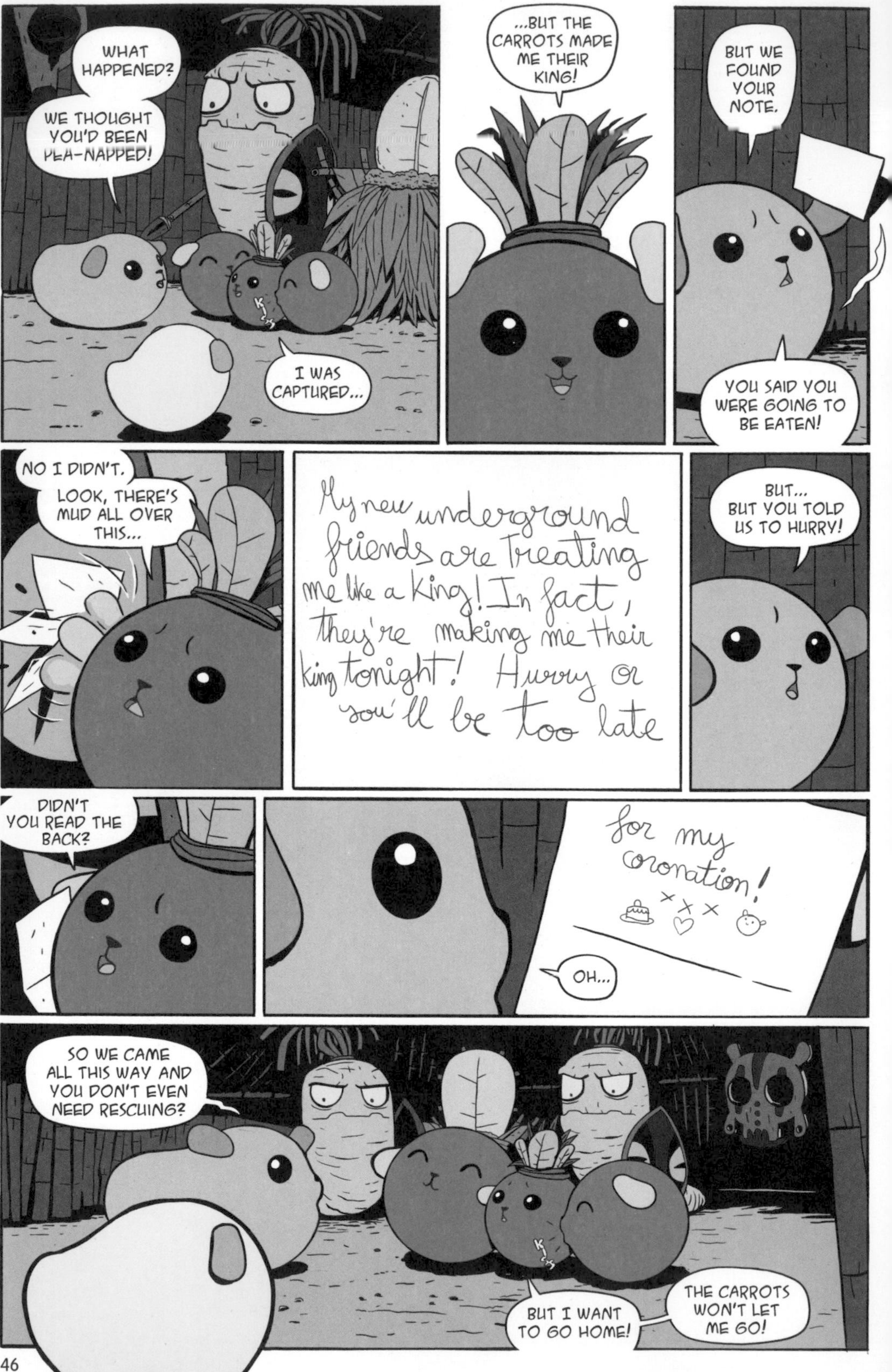
WHAT HAPPENED?
WE THOUGHT YOU'D BEEN PEA-NAPPED!
I WAS CAPTURED...
...BUT THE CARROTS MADE ME THEIR KING!
BUT WE FOUND YOUR NOTE.
YOU SAID YOU WERE GOING TO BE EATEN!
NO I DIDN'T.
LOOK, THERE'S MUD ALL OVER THIS...
My new underground friends are Treating me like a King! In fact, they're making me their King tonight! Hurry or you'll be too late
BUT... BUT YOU TOLD US TO HURRY!
DIDN'T YOU READ THE BACK?
for my coronation!
xxx
OH...
SO WE CAME ALL THIS WAY AND YOU DON'T EVEN NEED RESCUING?
BUT I WANT TO GO HOME!
THE CARROTS WON'T LET ME GO!

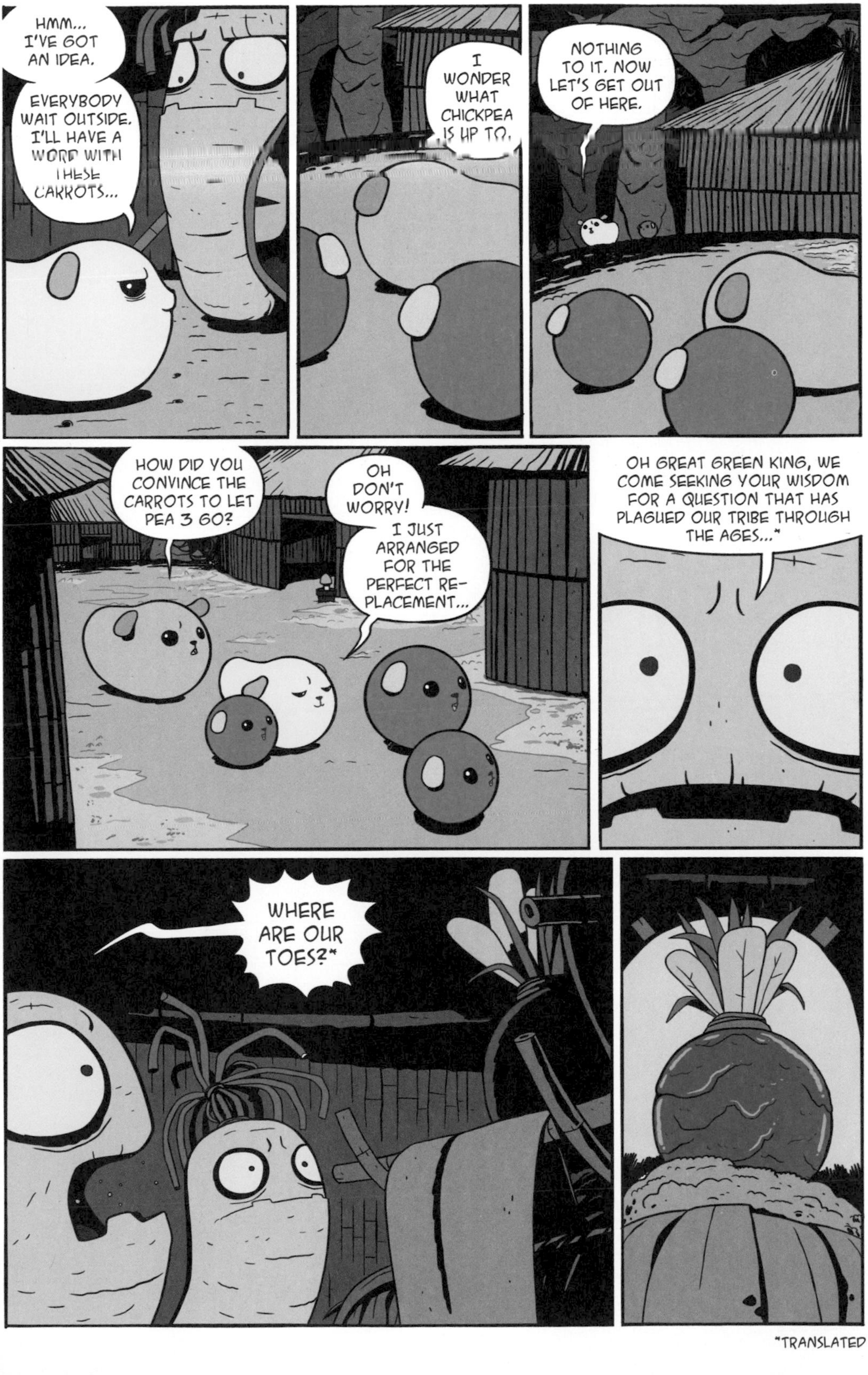
HMM... I'VE GOT AN IDEA.
EVERYBODY WAIT OUTSIDE. I'LL HAVE A WORD WITH THESE CARROTS...
I WONDER WHAT CHICKPEA IS UP TO.
NOTHING TO IT. NOW LET'S GET OUT OF HERE.
HOW DID YOU CONVINCE THE CARROTS TO LET PEA 3 GO?
OH DON'T WORRY!
I JUST ARRANGED FOR THE PERFECT RE-PLACEMENT...
OH GREAT GREEN KING, WE COME SEEKING YOUR WISDOM FOR A QUESTION THAT HAS PLAGUED OUR TRIBE THROUGH THE AGES...*
WHERE ARE OUR TOES?*
*TRANSLATED

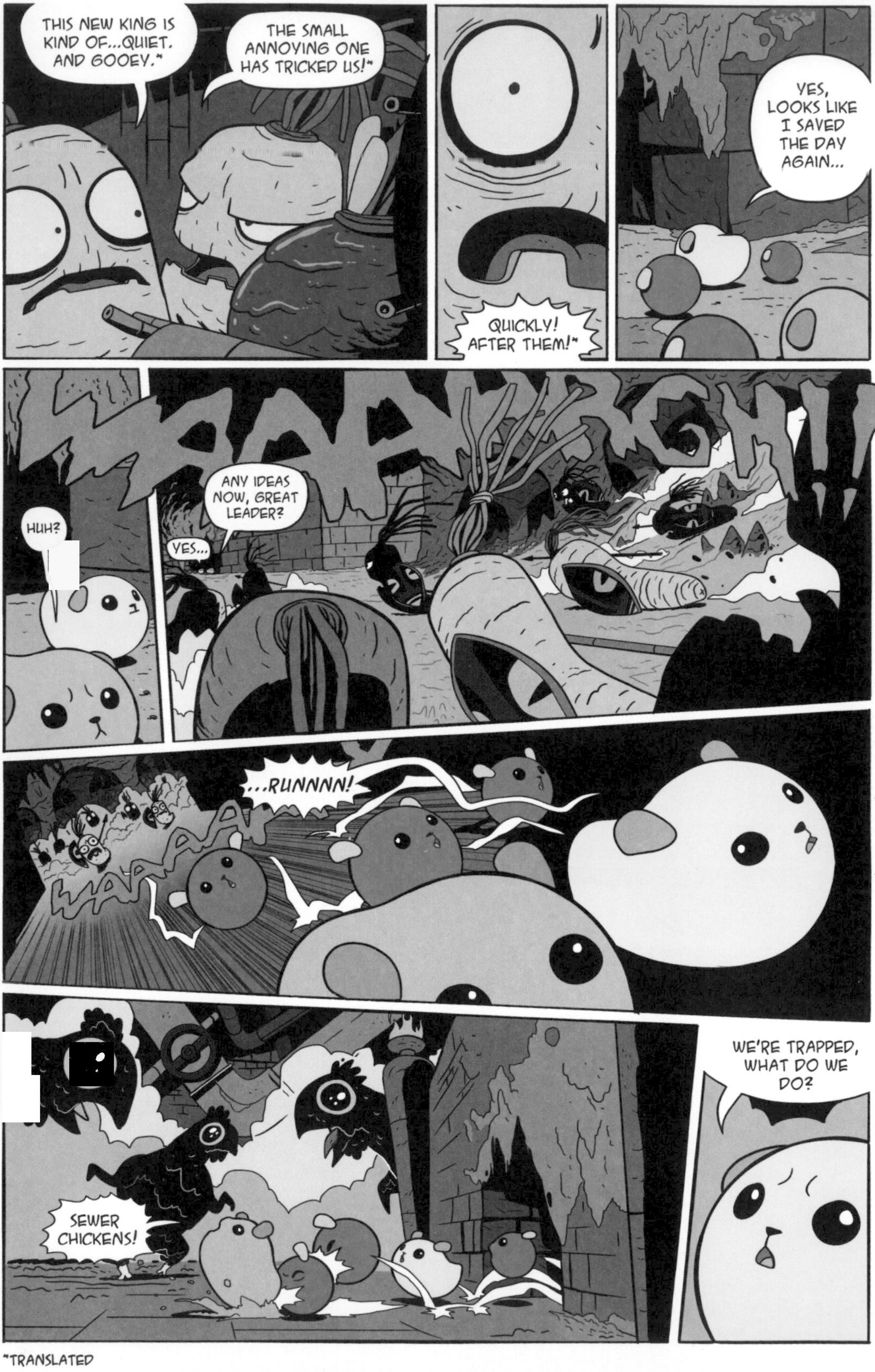
THIS NEW KING IS KIND OF...QUIET. AND GOOEY.*
THE SMALL ANNOYING ONE HAS TRICKED US!*
QUICKLY! AFTER THEM!*
YES, LOOKS LIKE I SAVED THE DAY AGAIN...
HUH?
ANY IDEAS NOW, GREAT LEADER?
YES...
...RUNNNN!
SEWER CHICKENS!
WE'RE TRAPPED, WHAT DO WE DO?

*TRANSLATED

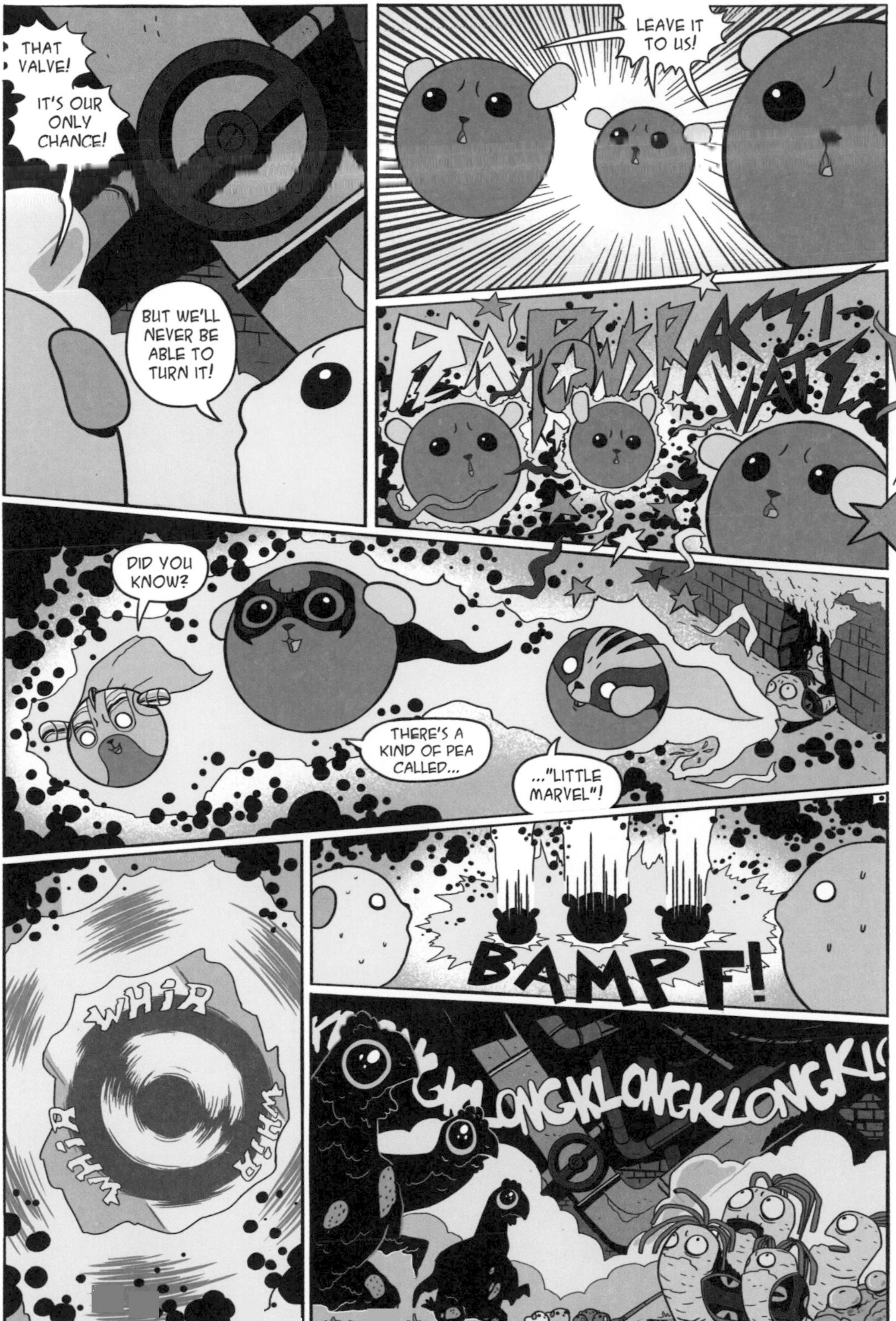
THAT VALVE!
IT'S OUR ONLY CHANCE!
BUT WE'LL NEVER BE ABLE TO TURN IT!
LEAVE IT TO US!
PEA POWER ACTIVATE!
DID YOU KNOW?
THERE'S A KIND OF PEA CALLED...
..."LITTLE MARVEL"!
WHIR
WHIR
WHIR
BAMPF!
KLONGKLONGKLONGKL

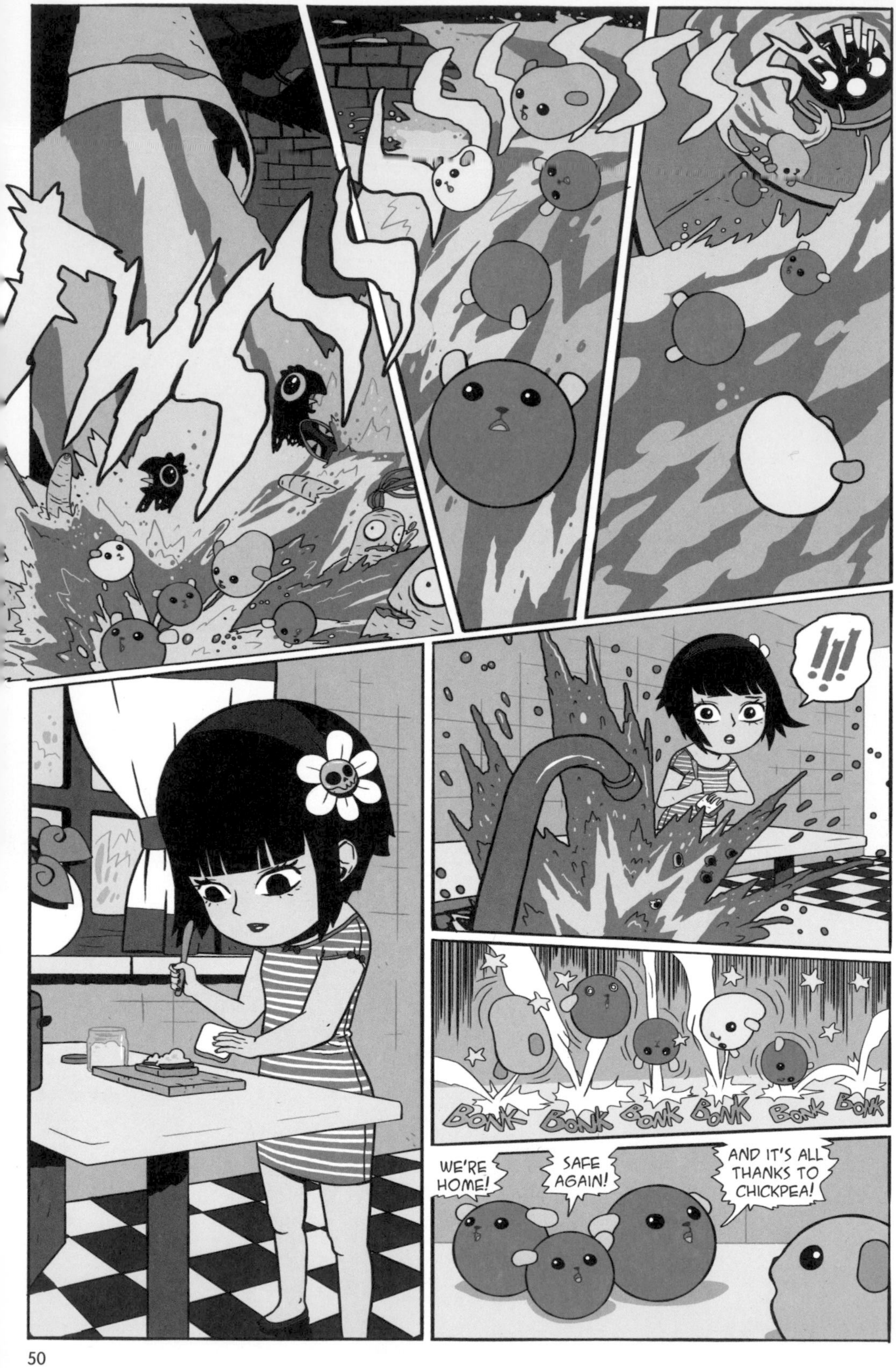

!!!
BONK BONK BONK BONK BONK BONK
WE'RE HOME!
SAFE AGAIN!
AND IT'S ALL THANKS TO CHICKPEA!

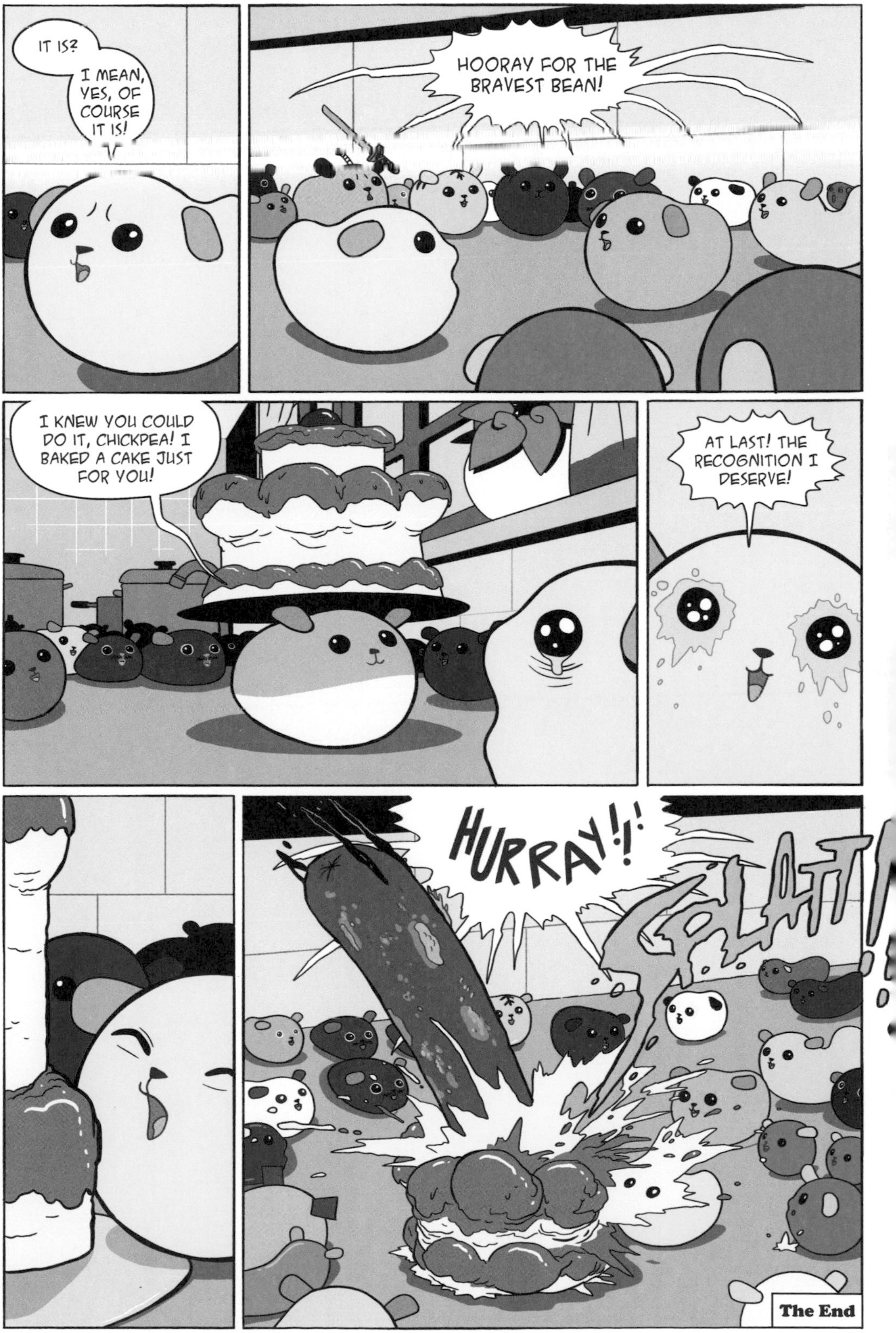
IT IS?
I MEAN, YES, OF COURSE IT IS!
HOORAY FOR THE BRAVEST BEAN!
I KNEW YOU COULD DO IT, CHICKPEA! I BAKED A CAKE JUST FOR YOU!
AT LAST! THE RECOGNITION I DESERVE!
HURRAY!!!
SPLATT!!
The End

mameshiba

On the LOOSE!

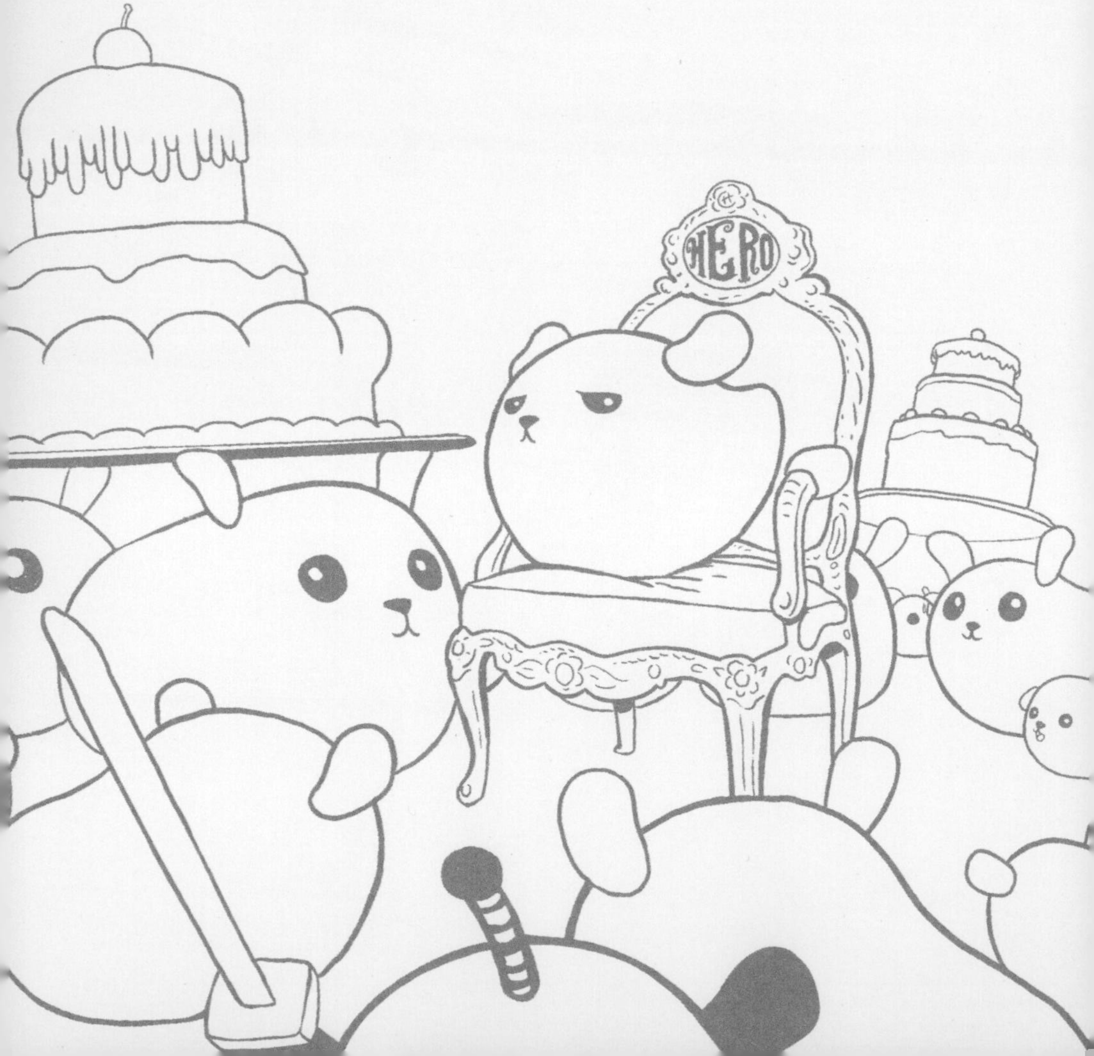
HERO

PISTACHIO WITH A heart

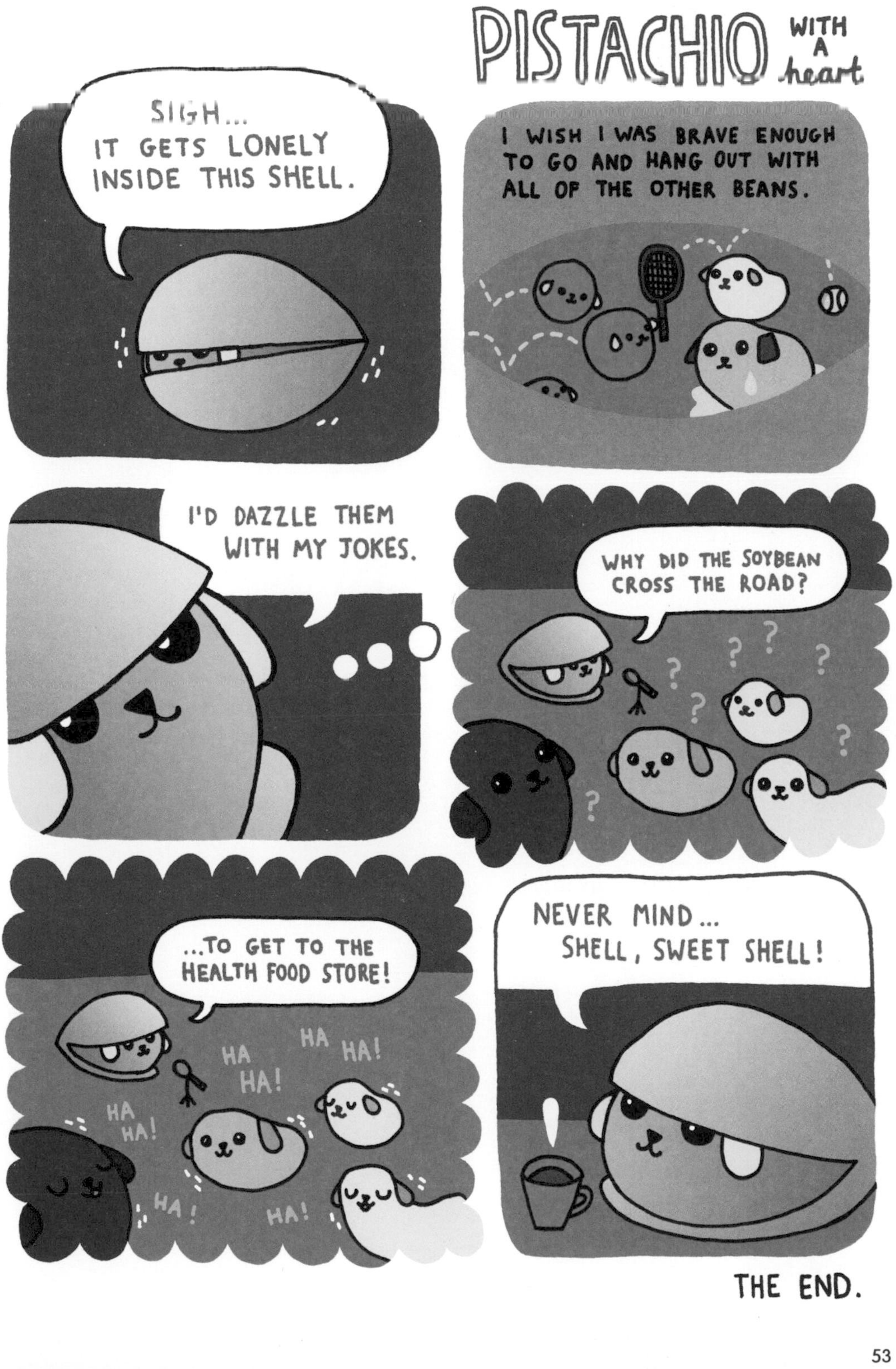
SIGH...
IT GETS LONELY
INSIDE THIS SHELL.
I WISH I WAS BRAVE ENOUGH
TO GO AND HANG OUT WITH
ALL OF THE OTHER BEANS.
I'D DAZZLE THEM
WITH MY JOKES.
WHY DID THE SOYBEAN
CROSS THE ROAD?
...TO GET TO THE
HEALTH FOOD STORE!
HA HA! HA HA! HA HA! HA! HA!
NEVER MIND...
SHELL, SWEET SHELL!

THE END.

mameshiba

On the LOOSE!

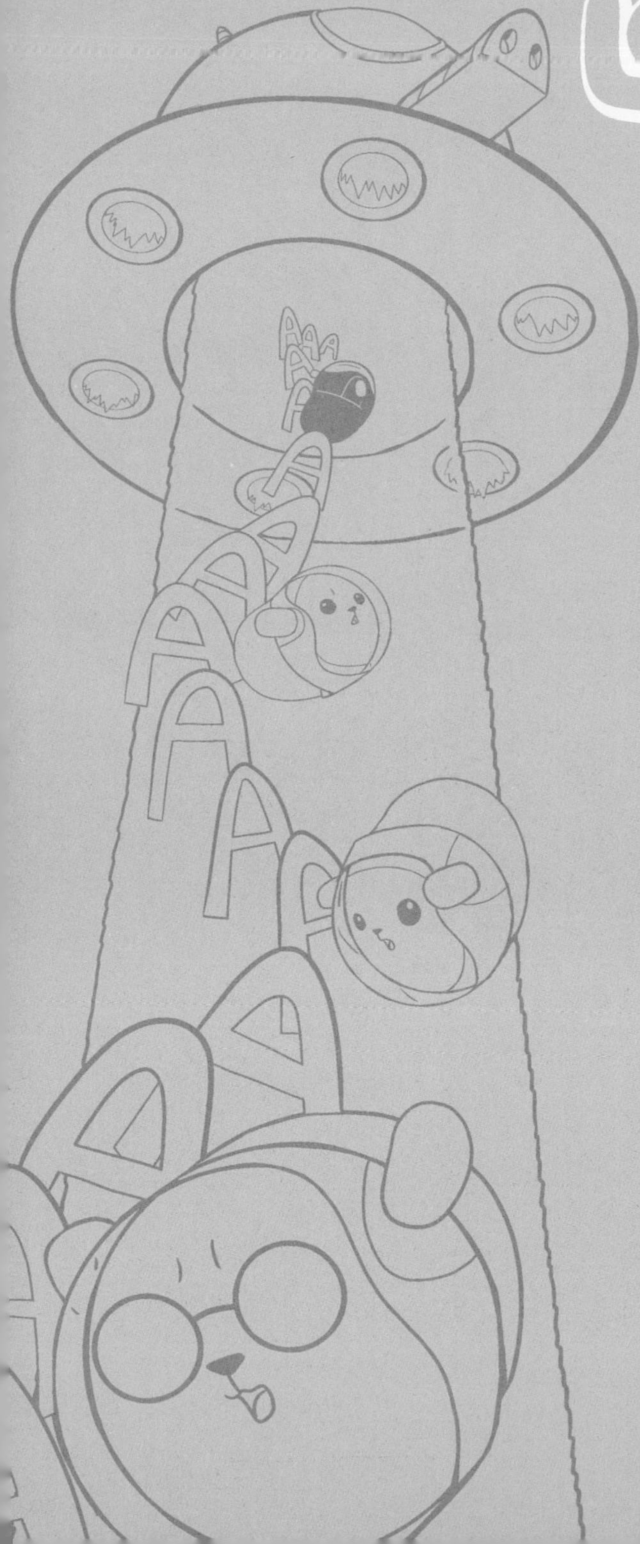

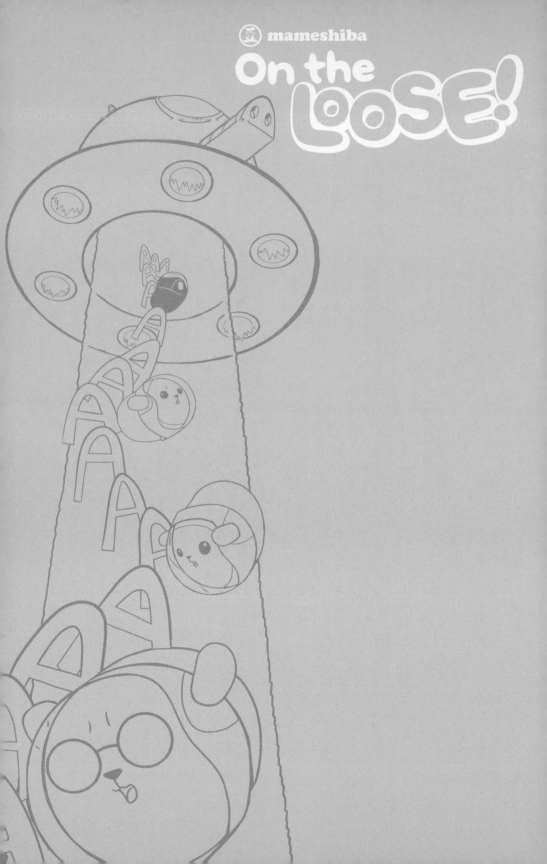

Planets and
Stuff

A bunch
of stars

Beans in
SPACE!

Moon

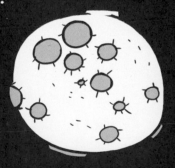

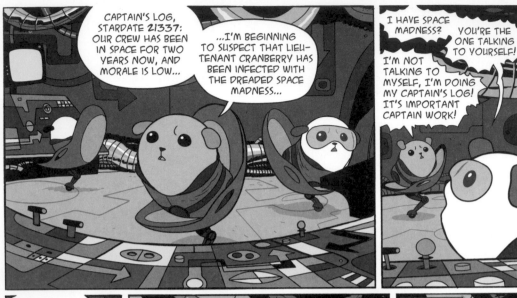

CAPTAIN'S LOG, STARDATE **21337**: OUR CREW HAS BEEN IN SPACE FOR TWO YEARS NOW, AND MORALE IS LOW...

...I'M BEGINNING TO SUSPECT THAT LIEU-TENANT CRANBERRY HAS BEEN INFECTED WITH THE DREADED SPACE MADNESS...

I HAVE SPACE MADNESS?

YOU'RE THE ONE TALKING TO YOURSELF!

I'M NOT TALKING TO MYSELF, I'M DOING MY CAPTAIN'S LOG! IT'S IMPORTANT CAPTAIN WORK!

PERHAPS IT'S BLACK-EYED PEA THAT HAS SPACE MADNESS, THEN...

MUSHROOMS!

HMM... POSSIBLY...

Suddenly!

CAPTAIN! WE'RE FLYING TOO CLOSE TO A BLACK HOLE! WE'RE ABOUT TO BE SUCKED IN!

QUICKLY! ACTIVATE THE BLACK HOLE REPULSION SHIELDS!

I CAN'T. BLACK-EYED PEA IS RIDING THEM LIKE A HORSEY.

WE'RE *DOOMED*.

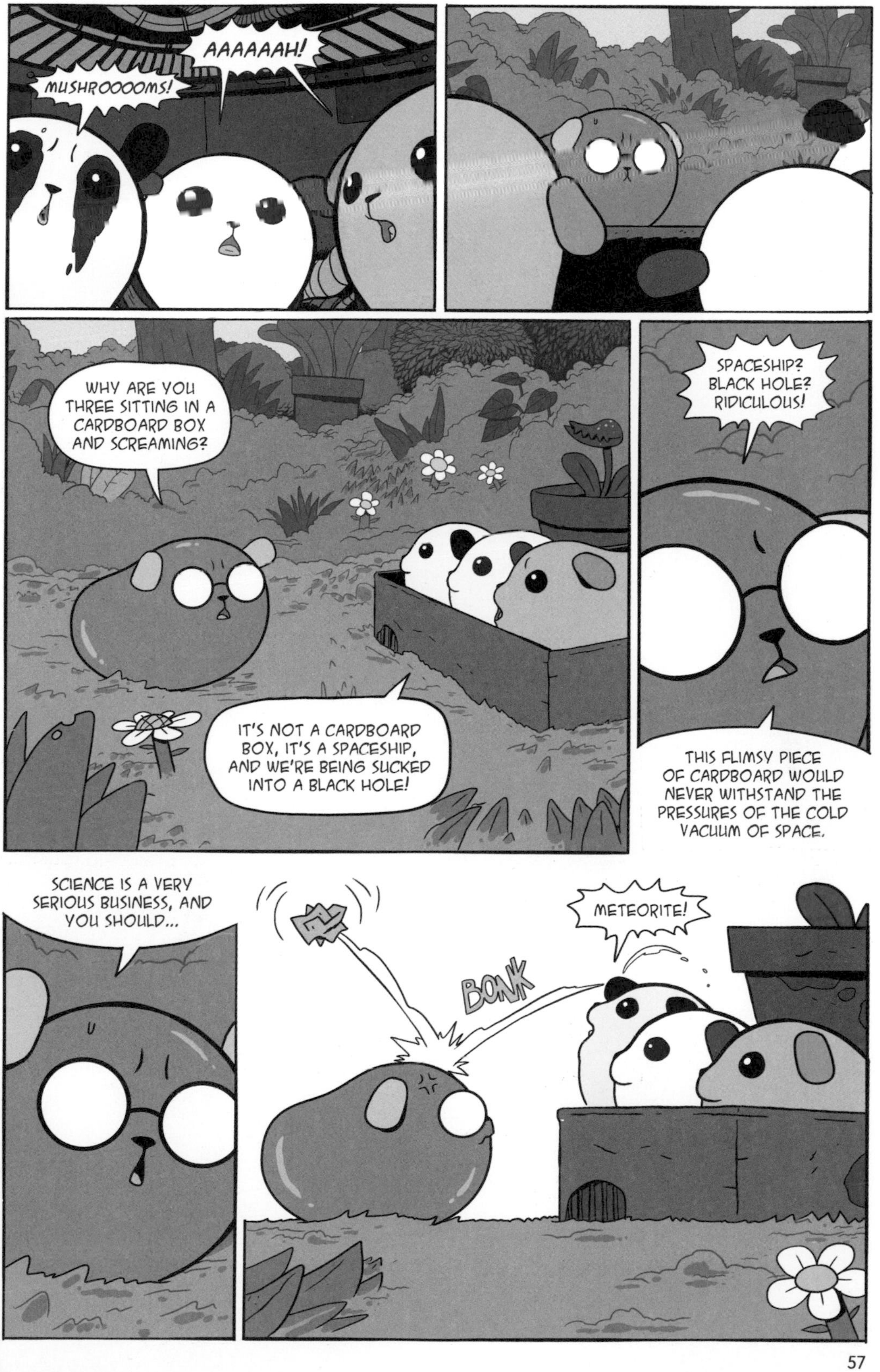

MUSHROOOOMS!
AAAAAAH!
WHY ARE YOU THREE SITTING IN A CARDBOARD BOX AND SCREAMING?
IT'S NOT A CARDBOARD BOX, IT'S A SPACESHIP, AND WE'RE BEING SUCKED INTO A BLACK HOLE!
SPACESHIP? BLACK HOLE? RIDICULOUS!
THIS FLIMSY PIECE OF CARDBOARD WOULD NEVER WITHSTAND THE PRESSURES OF THE COLD VACUUM OF SPACE.
SCIENCE IS A VERY SERIOUS BUSINESS, AND YOU SHOULD...
BONK
METEORITE!

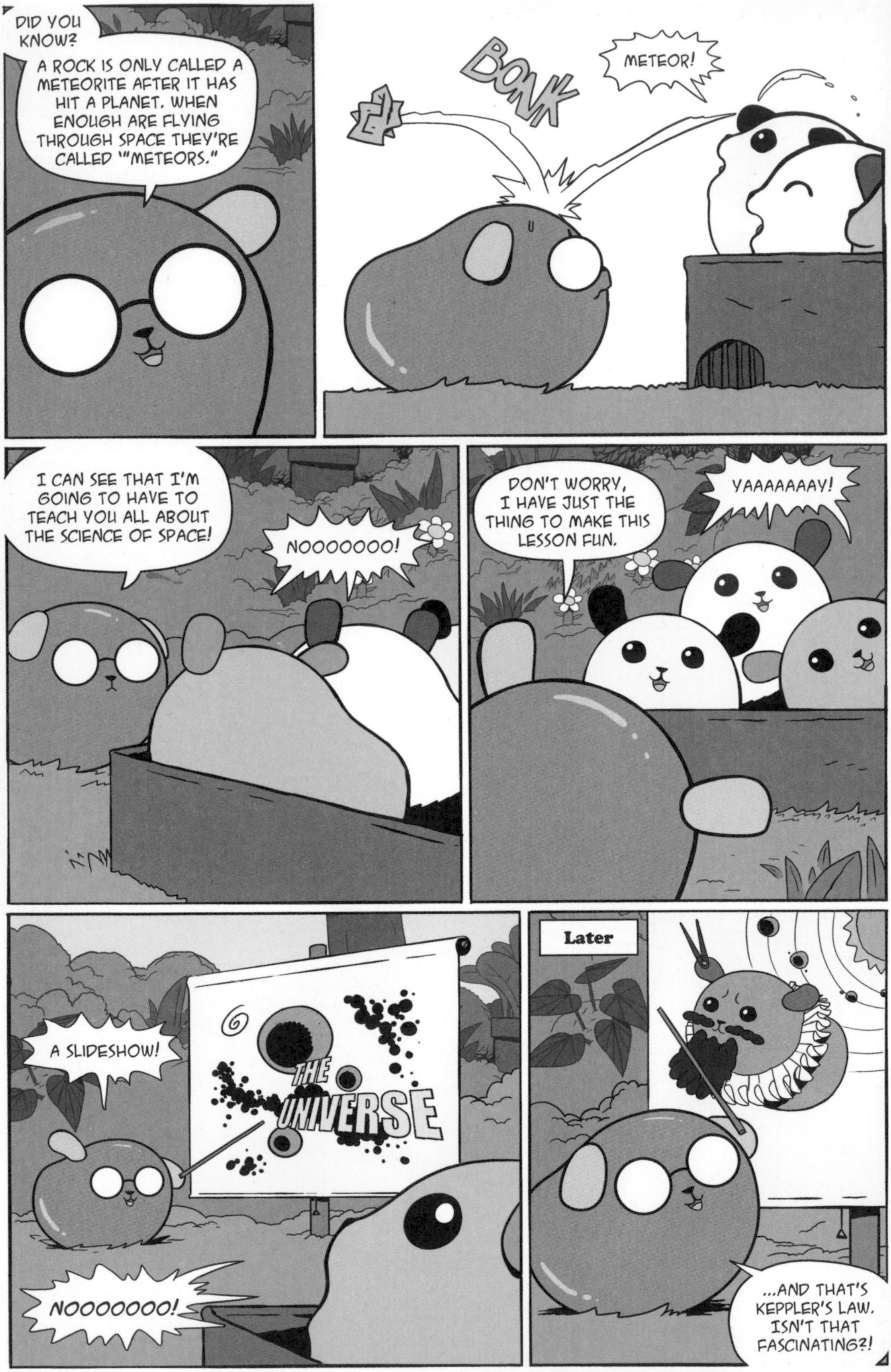
DID YOU KNOW?
A ROCK IS ONLY CALLED A METEORITE AFTER IT HAS HIT A PLANET. WHEN ENOUGH ARE FLYING THROUGH SPACE THEY'RE CALLED "METEORS."
BONK
METEOR!
I CAN SEE THAT I'M GOING TO HAVE TO TEACH YOU ALL ABOUT THE SCIENCE OF SPACE!
NOOOOOOO!
DON'T WORRY, I HAVE JUST THE THING TO MAKE THIS LESSON FUN.
YAAAAAAAY!
A SLIDESHOW!
THE UNIVERSE
NOOOOOOO!
Later
...AND THAT'S KEPPLER'S LAW. ISN'T THAT FASCINATING?!

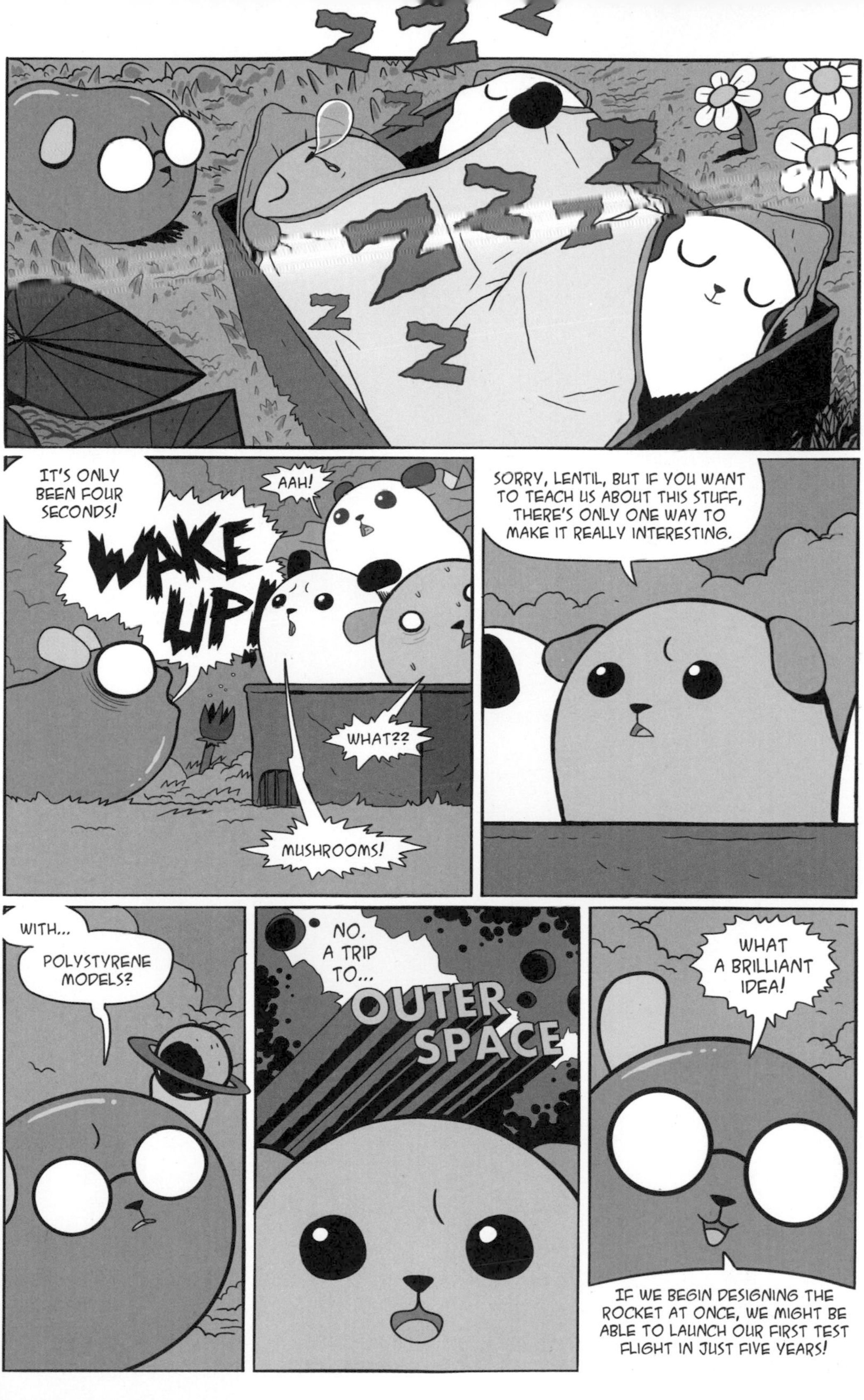
IT'S ONLY BEEN FOUR SECONDS!
WAKE UP!
AAH!
WHAT??
MUSHROOMS!
SORRY, LENTIL, BUT IF YOU WANT TO TEACH US ABOUT THIS STUFF, THERE'S ONLY ONE WAY TO MAKE IT REALLY INTERESTING.
WITH...
POLYSTYRENE MODELS?
NO. A TRIP TO...
OUTER SPACE
WHAT A BRILLIANT IDEA!
IF WE BEGIN DESIGNING THE ROCKET AT ONCE, WE MIGHT BE ABLE TO LAUNCH OUR FIRST TEST FLIGHT IN JUST FIVE YEARS!

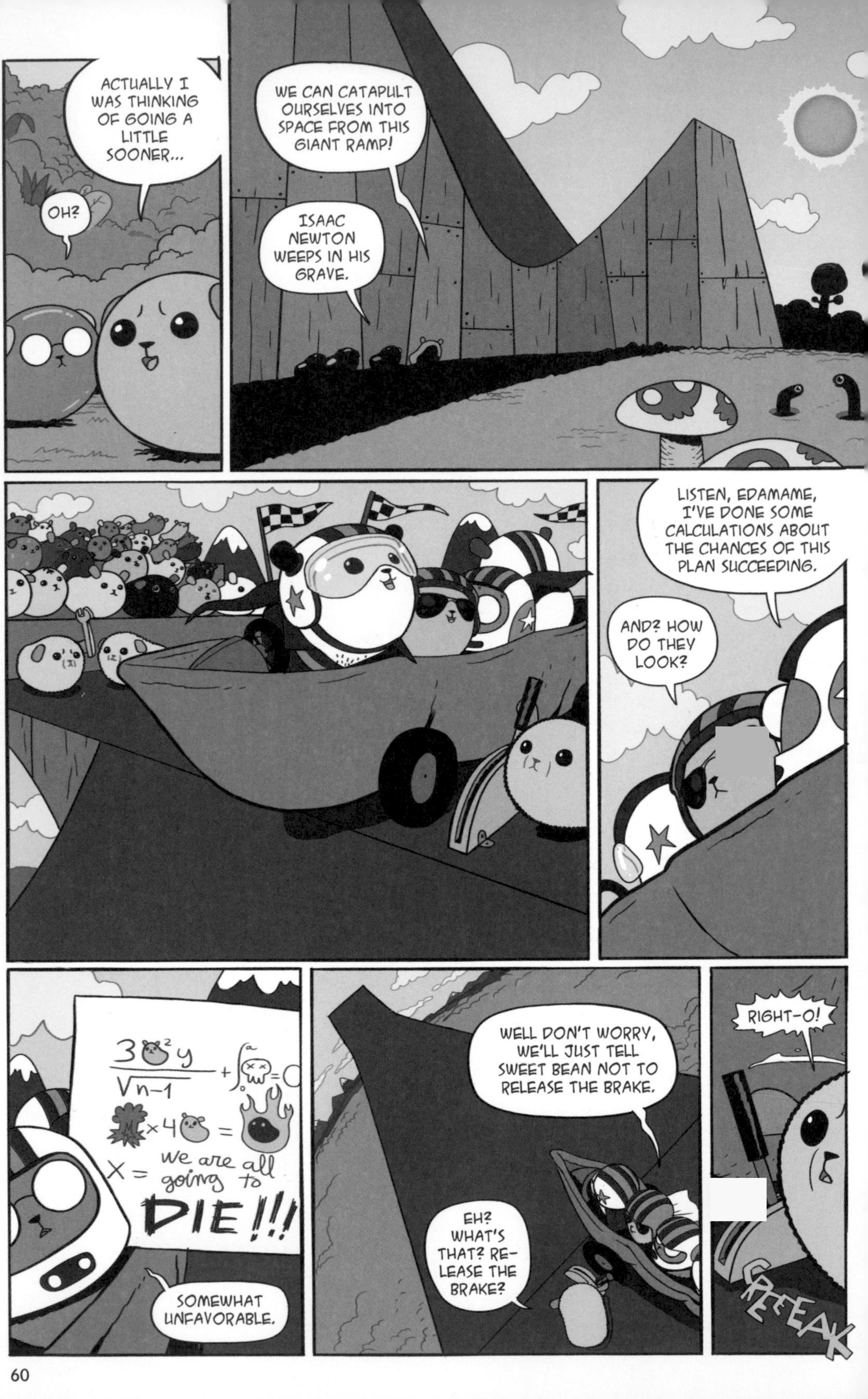
ACTUALLY I WAS THINKING OF GOING A LITTLE SOONER...
OH?
WE CAN CATAPULT OURSELVES INTO SPACE FROM THIS GIANT RAMP!
ISAAC NEWTON WEEPS IN HIS GRAVE.
LISTEN, EDAMAME, I'VE DONE SOME CALCULATIONS ABOUT THE CHANCES OF THIS PLAN SUCCEEDING.
AND? HOW DO THEY LOOK?
3 2 y
Vn−1
x4 =
X = we are all going to DIE!!!
SOMEWHAT UNFAVORABLE.
WELL DON'T WORRY, WE'LL JUST TELL SWEET BEAN NOT TO RELEASE THE BRAKE.
EH? WHAT'S THAT? RE-LEASE THE BRAKE?
RIGHT-O!
CREEEAK

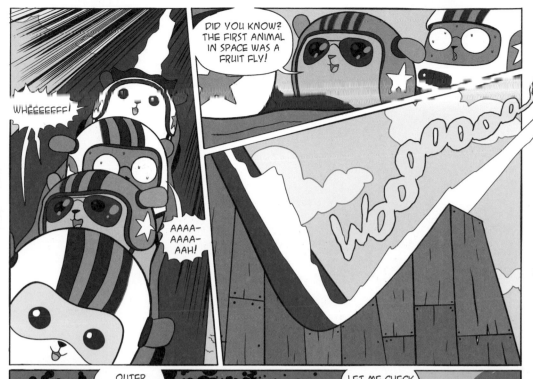

WHEEEEEEE!

DID YOU KNOW? THE FIRST ANIMAL IN SPACE WAS A FRUIT FLY!

AAAA-AAAA-AAH!

WooOoooo

OUTER SPACE, HERE WE COME!

LET ME CHECK THE MAP...

WHERE SHALL WE GO FIRST?

S P A C E

Moon

Planets and stuff

A bunch of stars

HOW ABOUT THE MOON?

ALRIGHT, HANG ON TO YOUR HELMETS!

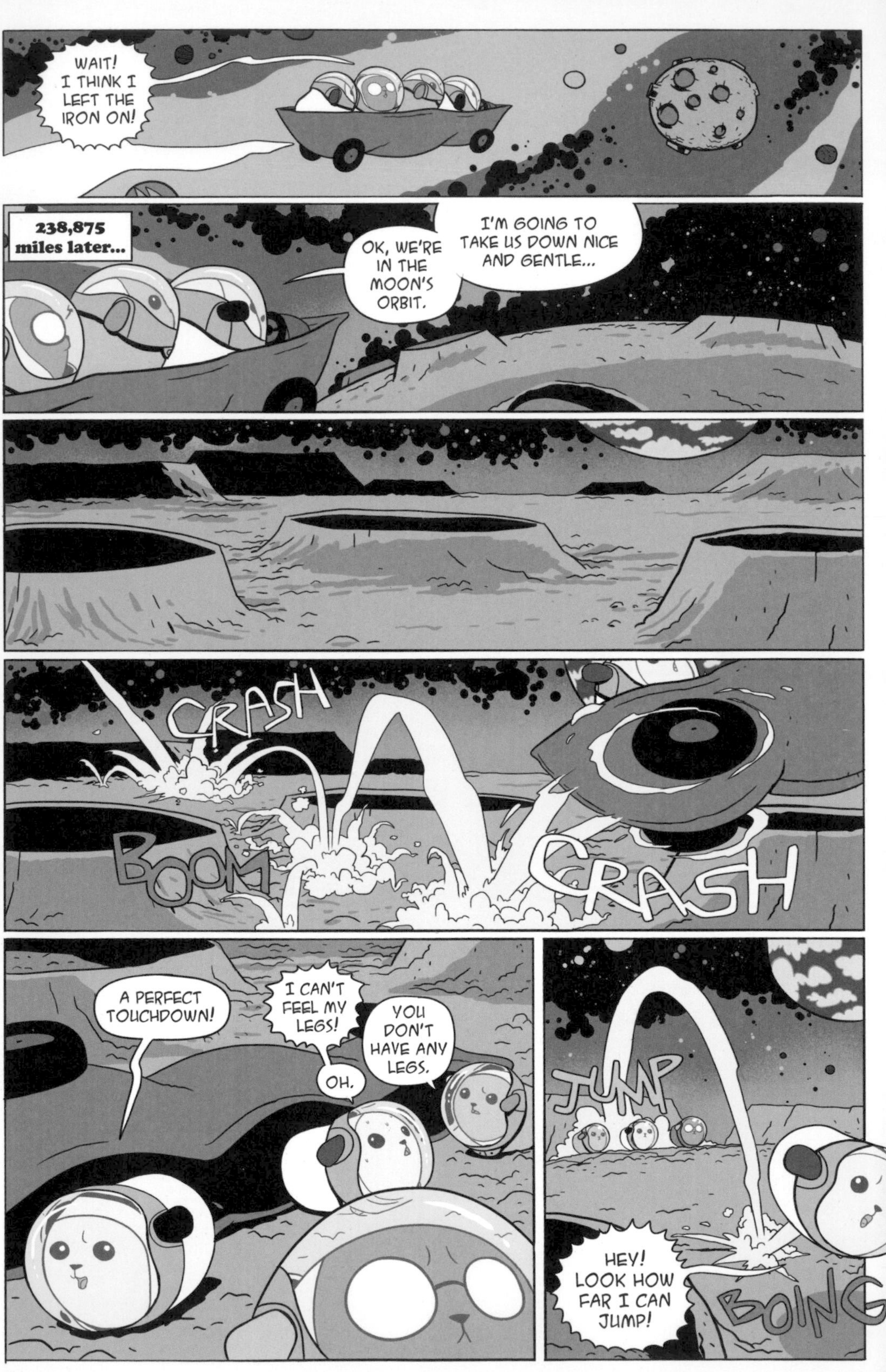
WAIT! I THINK I LEFT THE IRON ON!
238,875 miles later...
OK, WE'RE IN THE MOON'S ORBIT.
I'M GOING TO TAKE US DOWN NICE AND GENTLE...
CRASH
BOOM
CRASH
A PERFECT TOUCHDOWN!
I CAN'T FEEL MY LEGS!
YOU DON'T HAVE ANY LEGS.
OH.
JUMP
HEY! LOOK HOW FAR I CAN JUMP!
BOING

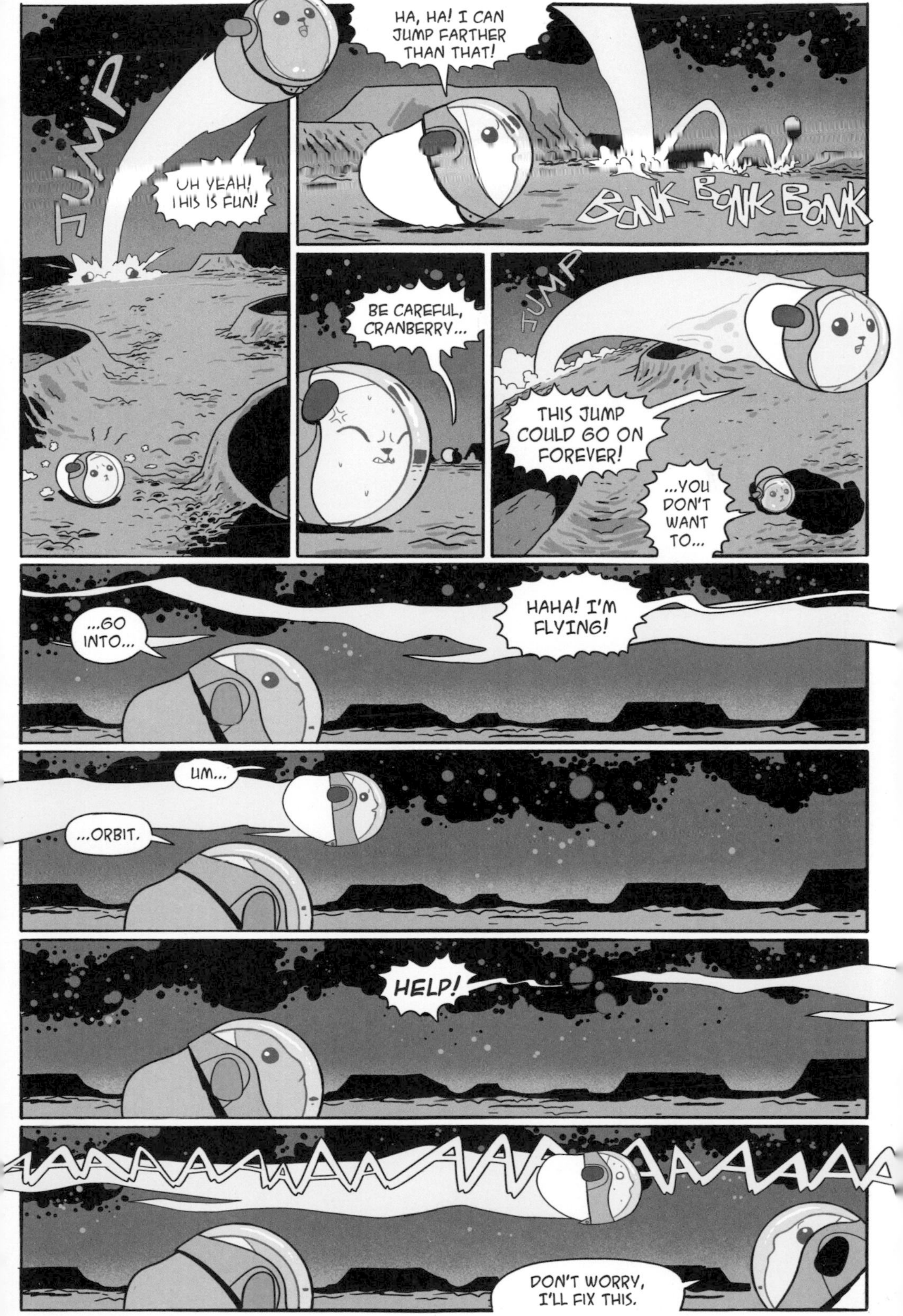
JUMP
UH YEAH! THIS IS FUN!
HA, HA! I CAN JUMP FARTHER THAN THAT!
BONK BONK BONK
BE CAREFUL, CRANBERRY...
JUMP
THIS JUMP COULD GO ON FOREVER!
...YOU DON'T WANT TO...
...GO INTO...
HAHA! I'M FLYING!
UM...
...ORBIT.
HELP!
AAAAAAAAAAAAAAAAAAA
DON'T WORRY, I'LL FIX THIS.

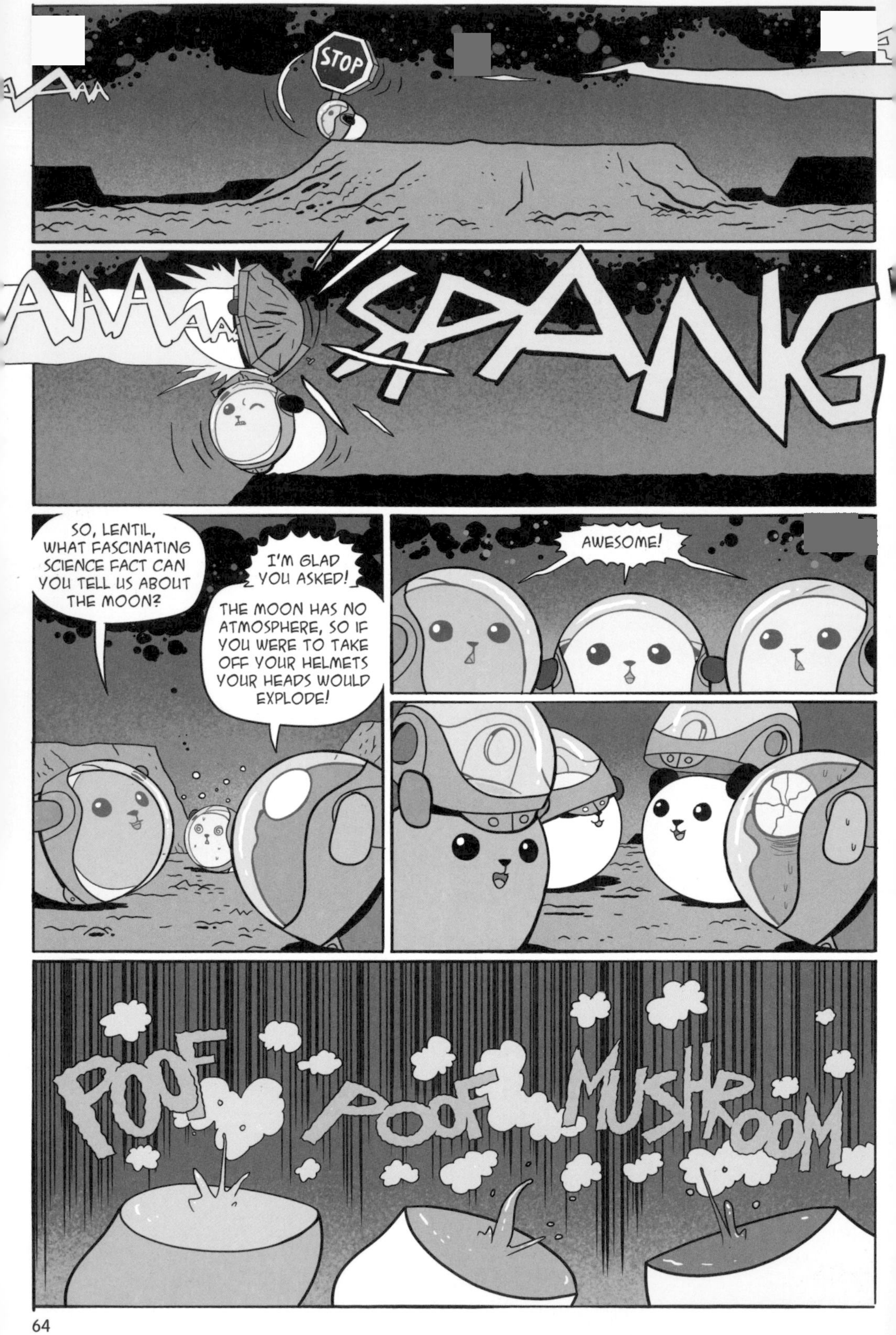
STOP
SPANG
SO, LENTIL, WHAT FASCINATING SCIENCE FACT CAN YOU TELL US ABOUT THE MOON?
I'M GLAD YOU ASKED!
THE MOON HAS NO ATMOSPHERE, SO IF YOU WERE TO TAKE OFF YOUR HELMETS YOUR HEADS WOULD EXPLODE!
AWESOME!
POOF
POOF
MUSHROOM

THAT WAS SO COOL!
YOU WERE RIGHT,
SCIENCE IS FUN!
WHERE SHOULD WE GO NEXT?
OOH, HOW ABOUT MARS! THE RED PLANET!
EXCELLENT IDEA! WHAT IS IT ABOUT MARS THAT INTERESTS YOU?
ITS SIMILARITY TO EARTH? ITS VARIED TERRAIN? ITS FROZEN SECRETS?
I JUST LIKE THE COLOR RED!
OH YES, IT'S THE RED-DEST COLOR!
WATCH OUT, MARS, HERE WE COME!
MAYBE I COULD JUST STAY HERE...
DID YOU KNOW?
THERE ARE BAGS OF ASTRONAUT POOP ON THE MOON THAT HAVE BEEN THERE SINCE THE FIRST MOON LANDING, MORE THAN 50 YEARS AGO.

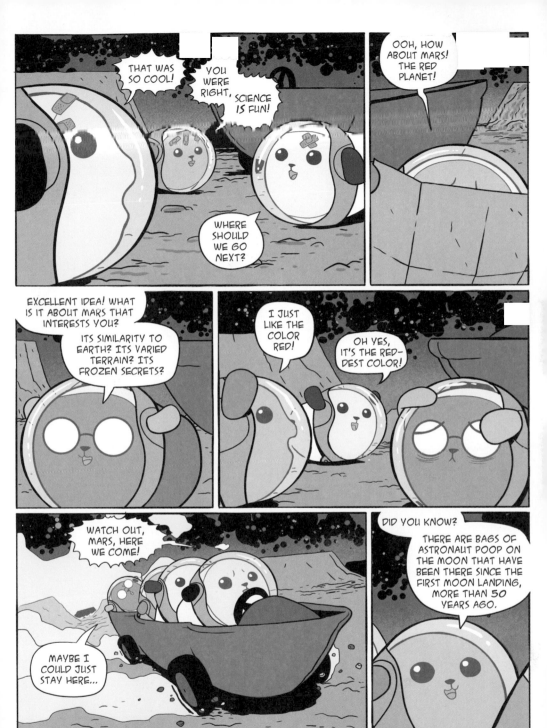

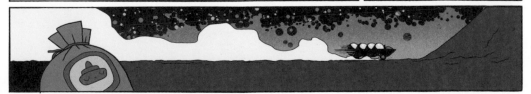

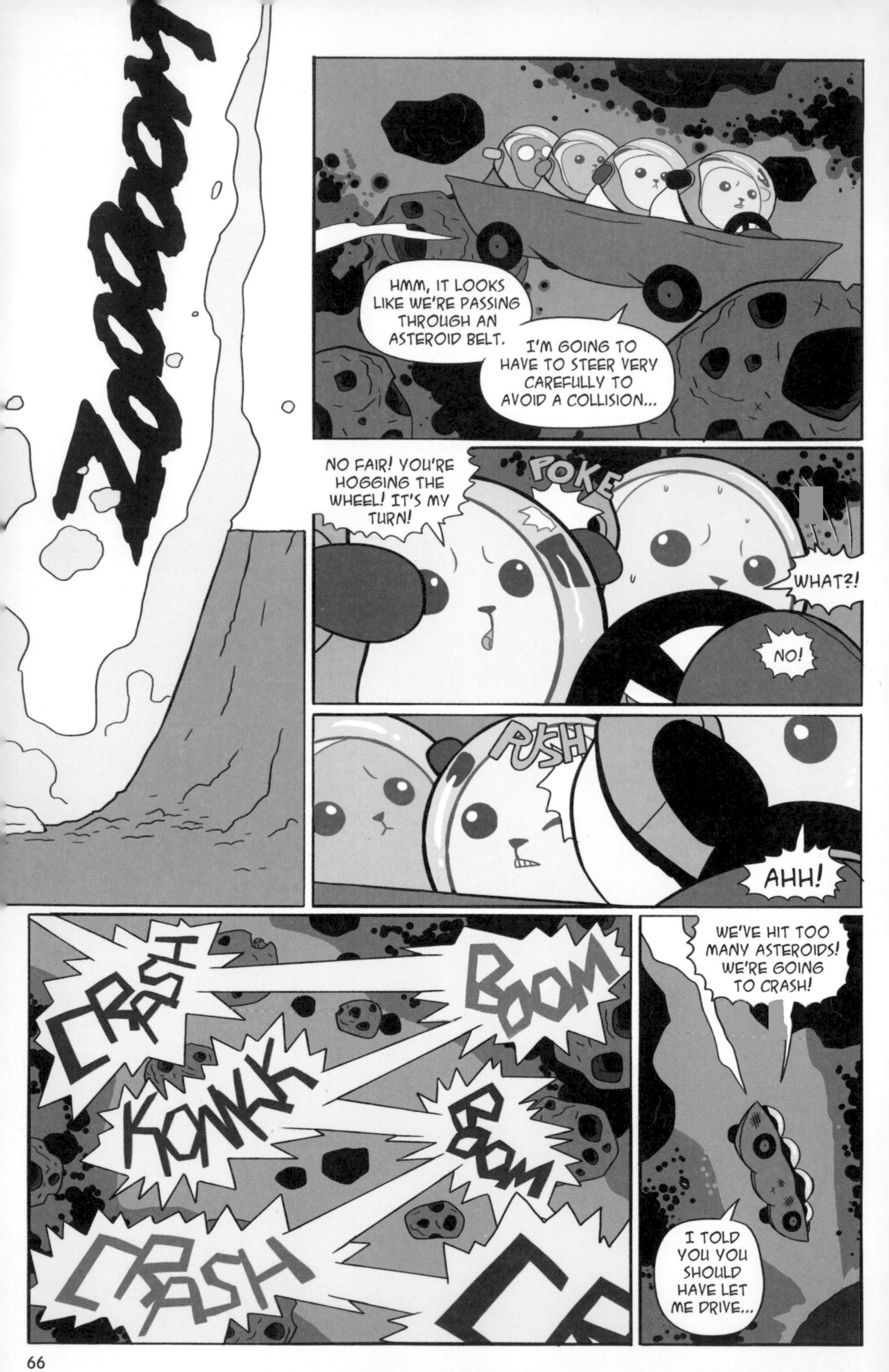
ZOOOOM
HMM, IT LOOKS LIKE WE'RE PASSING THROUGH AN ASTEROID BELT.
I'M GOING TO HAVE TO STEER VERY CAREFULLY TO AVOID A COLLISION...
NO FAIR! YOU'RE HOGGING THE WHEEL! IT'S MY TURN!
POKE
WHAT?!
NO!
AHH!
CRASH
BOOM
KONK
BOOM
CRASH
WE'VE HIT TOO MANY ASTEROIDS! WE'RE GOING TO CRASH!
I TOLD YOU YOU SHOULD HAVE LET ME DRIVE...

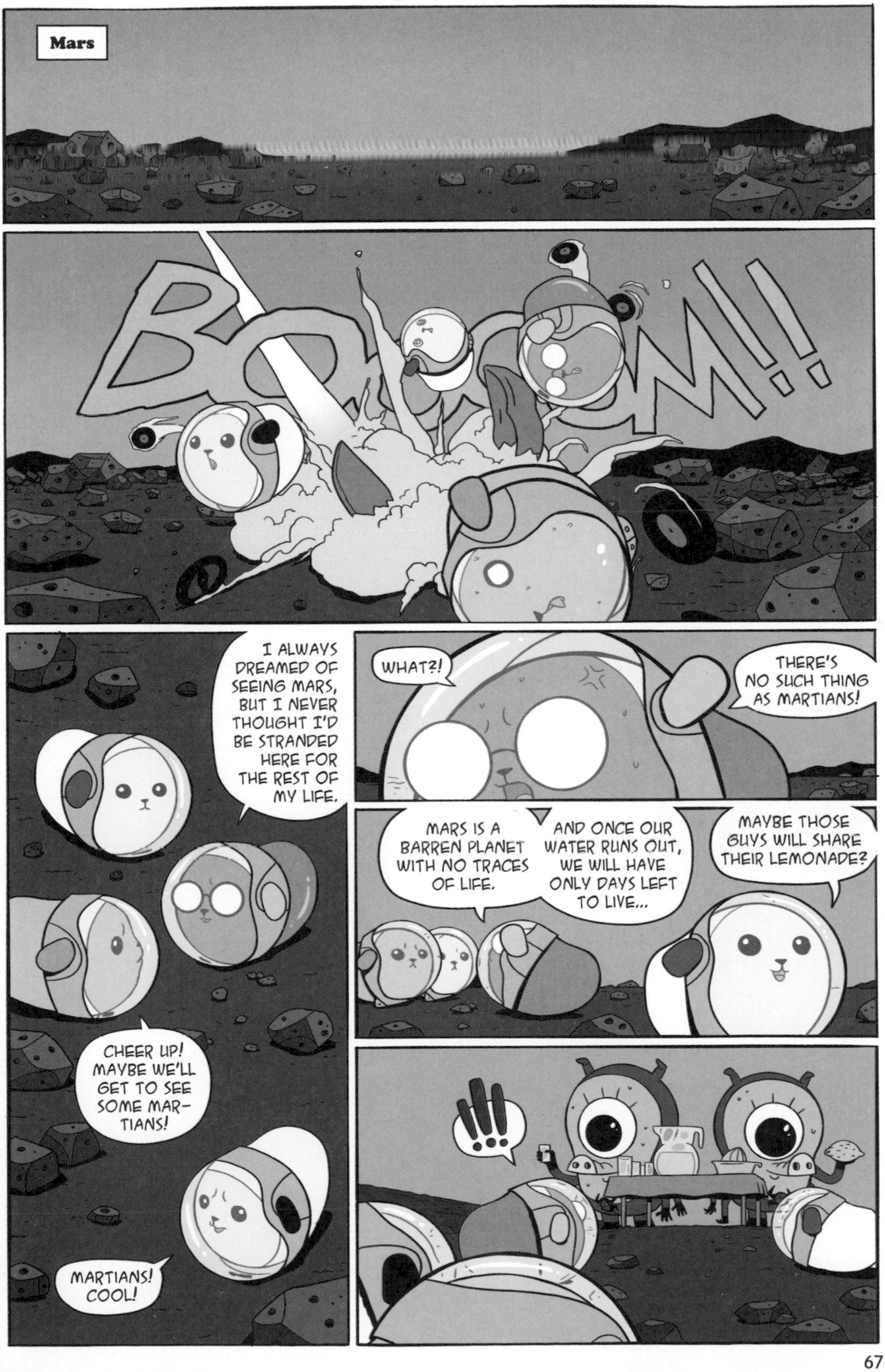
Mars
BOOM!!
I ALWAYS DREAMED OF SEEING MARS, BUT I NEVER THOUGHT I'D BE STRANDED HERE FOR THE REST OF MY LIFE.
CHEER UP! MAYBE WE'LL GET TO SEE SOME MAR- TIANS!
MARTIANS! COOL!
WHAT?!
THERE'S NO SUCH THING AS MARTIANS!
MARS IS A BARREN PLANET WITH NO TRACES OF LIFE.
AND ONCE OUR WATER RUNS OUT, WE WILL HAVE ONLY DAYS LEFT TO LIVE...
MAYBE THOSE GUYS WILL SHARE THEIR LEMONADE?
!!!

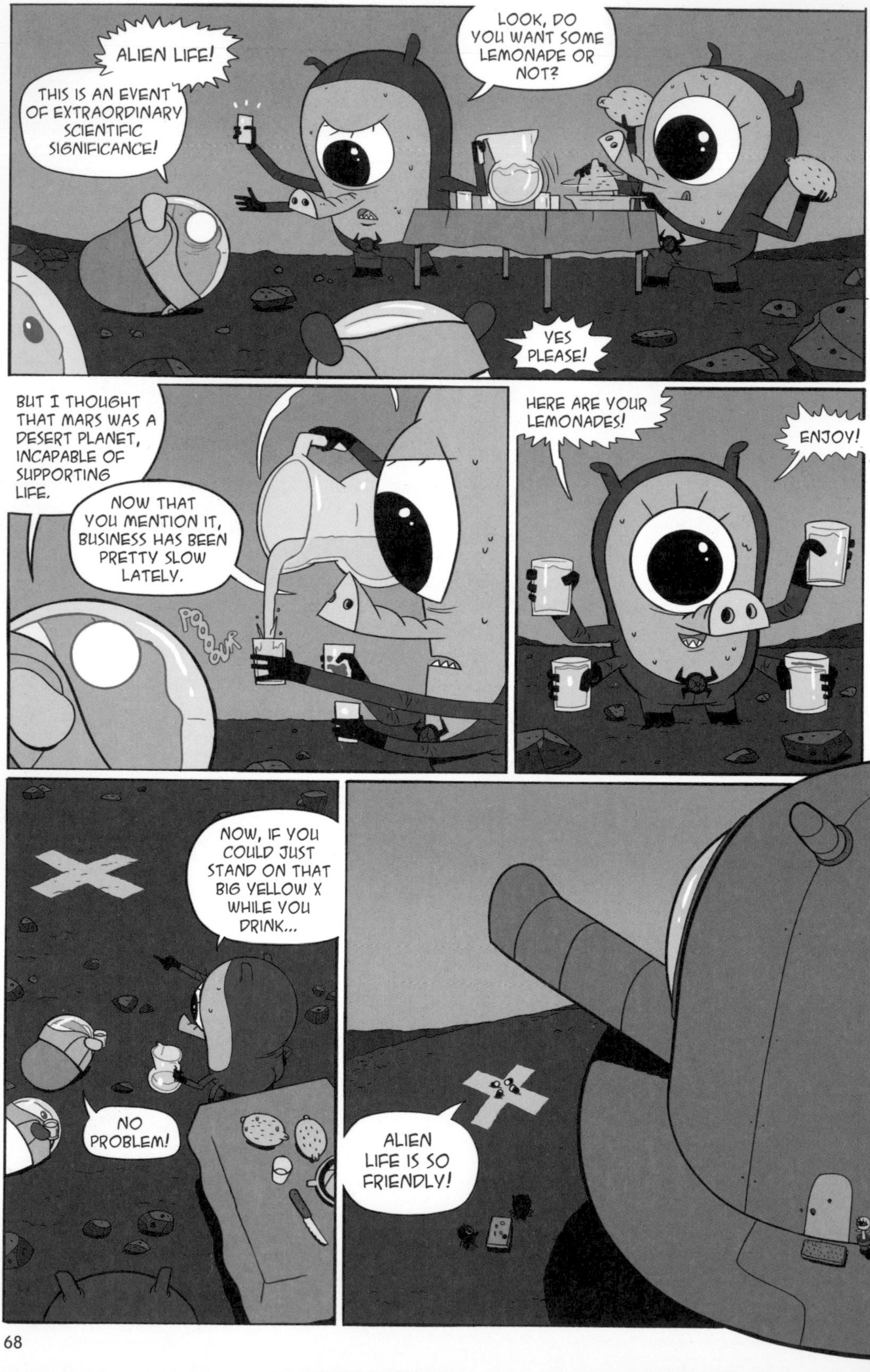
ALIEN LIFE!
THIS IS AN EVENT OF EXTRAORDINARY SCIENTIFIC SIGNIFICANCE!
LOOK, DO YOU WANT SOME LEMONADE OR NOT?
YES PLEASE!
BUT I THOUGHT THAT MARS WAS A DESERT PLANET, INCAPABLE OF SUPPORTING LIFE.
NOW THAT YOU MENTION IT, BUSINESS HAS BEEN PRETTY SLOW LATELY.
POOOUR
HERE ARE YOUR LEMONADES!
ENJOY!
NOW, IF YOU COULD JUST STAND ON THAT BIG YELLOW X WHILE YOU DRINK...
NO PROBLEM!
ALIEN LIFE IS SO FRIENDLY!

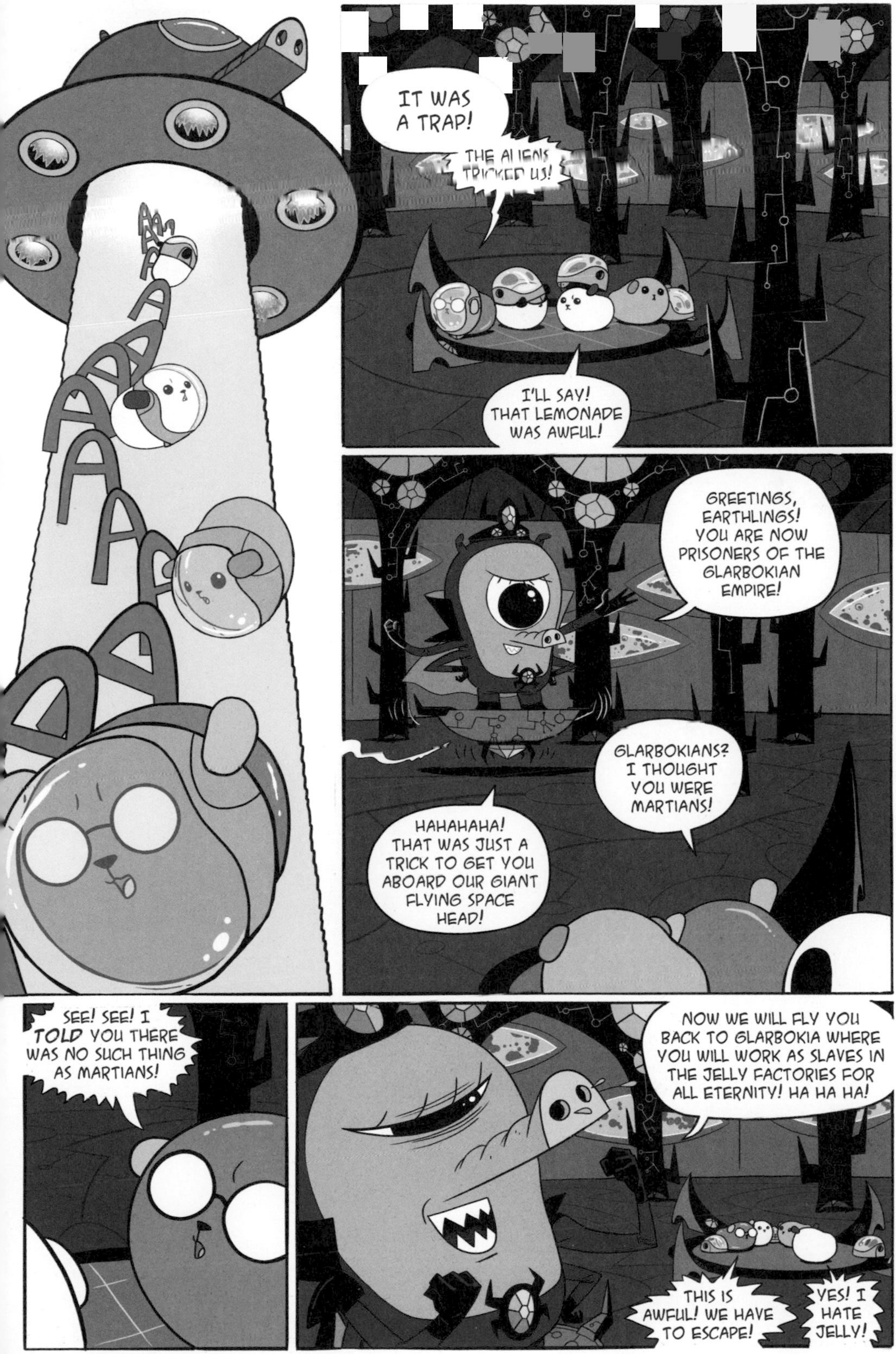
AAAAAAAAAAAA
IT WAS A TRAP!
THE ALIENS TRICKED US!
I'LL SAY! THAT LEMONADE WAS AWFUL!
GREETINGS, EARTHLINGS! YOU ARE NOW PRISONERS OF THE GLARBOKIAN EMPIRE!
GLARBOKIANS? I THOUGHT YOU WERE MARTIANS!
HAHAHAHA! THAT WAS JUST A TRICK TO GET YOU ABOARD OUR GIANT FLYING SPACE HEAD!
SEE! SEE! I *TOLD* YOU THERE WAS NO SUCH THING AS MARTIANS!
NOW WE WILL FLY YOU BACK TO GLARBOKIA WHERE YOU WILL WORK AS SLAVES IN THE JELLY FACTORIES FOR ALL ETERNITY! HA HA HA!
THIS IS AWFUL! WE HAVE TO ESCAPE!
YES! I HATE JELLY!

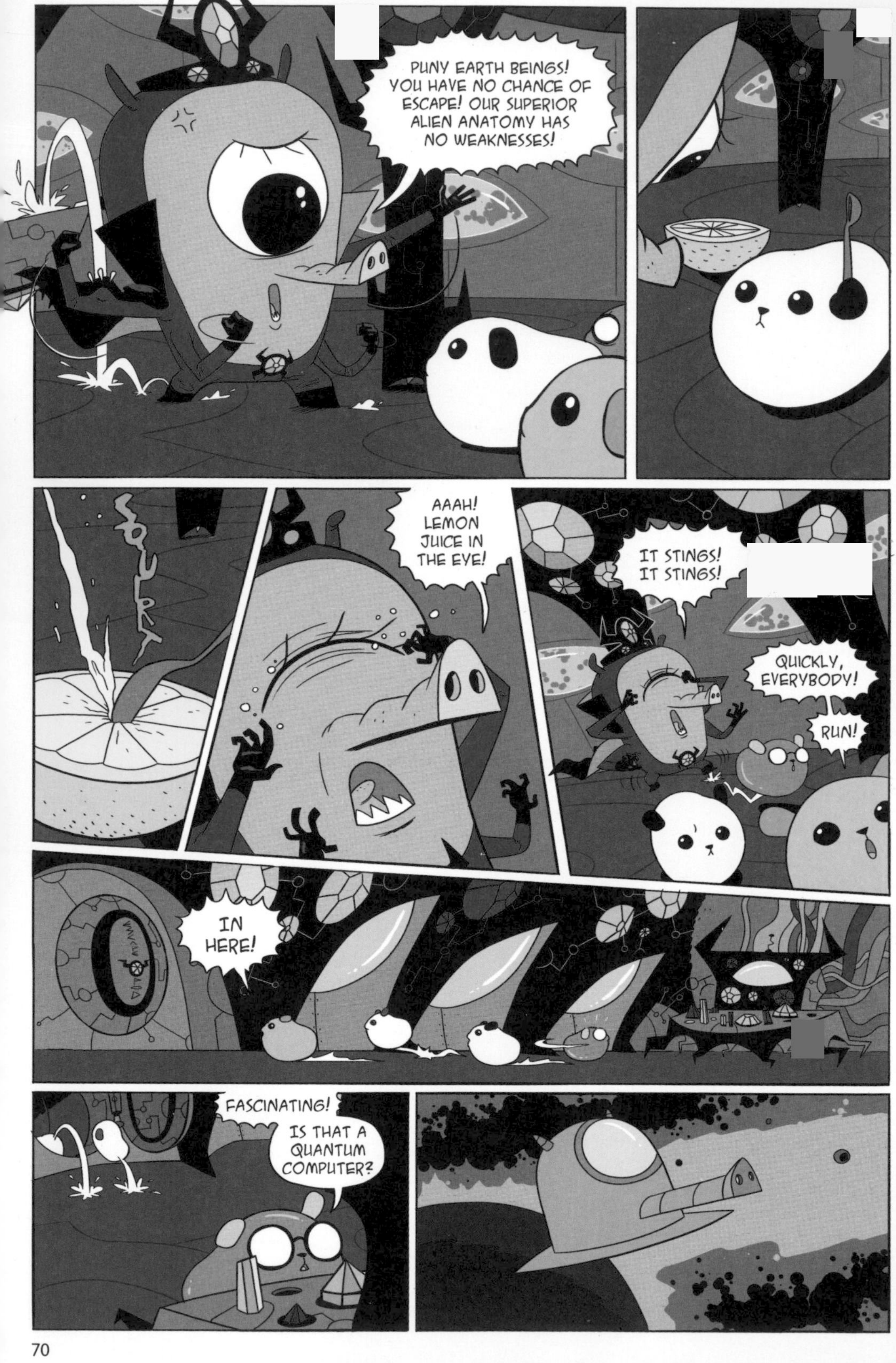
PUNY EARTH BEINGS! YOU HAVE NO CHANCE OF ESCAPE! OUR SUPERIOR ALIEN ANATOMY HAS NO WEAKNESSES!
SQUIRT
AAAH! LEMON JUICE IN THE EYE!
IT STINGS! IT STINGS!
QUICKLY, EVERYBODY!
RUN!
IN HERE!
FASCINATING!
IS THAT A QUANTUM COMPUTER?

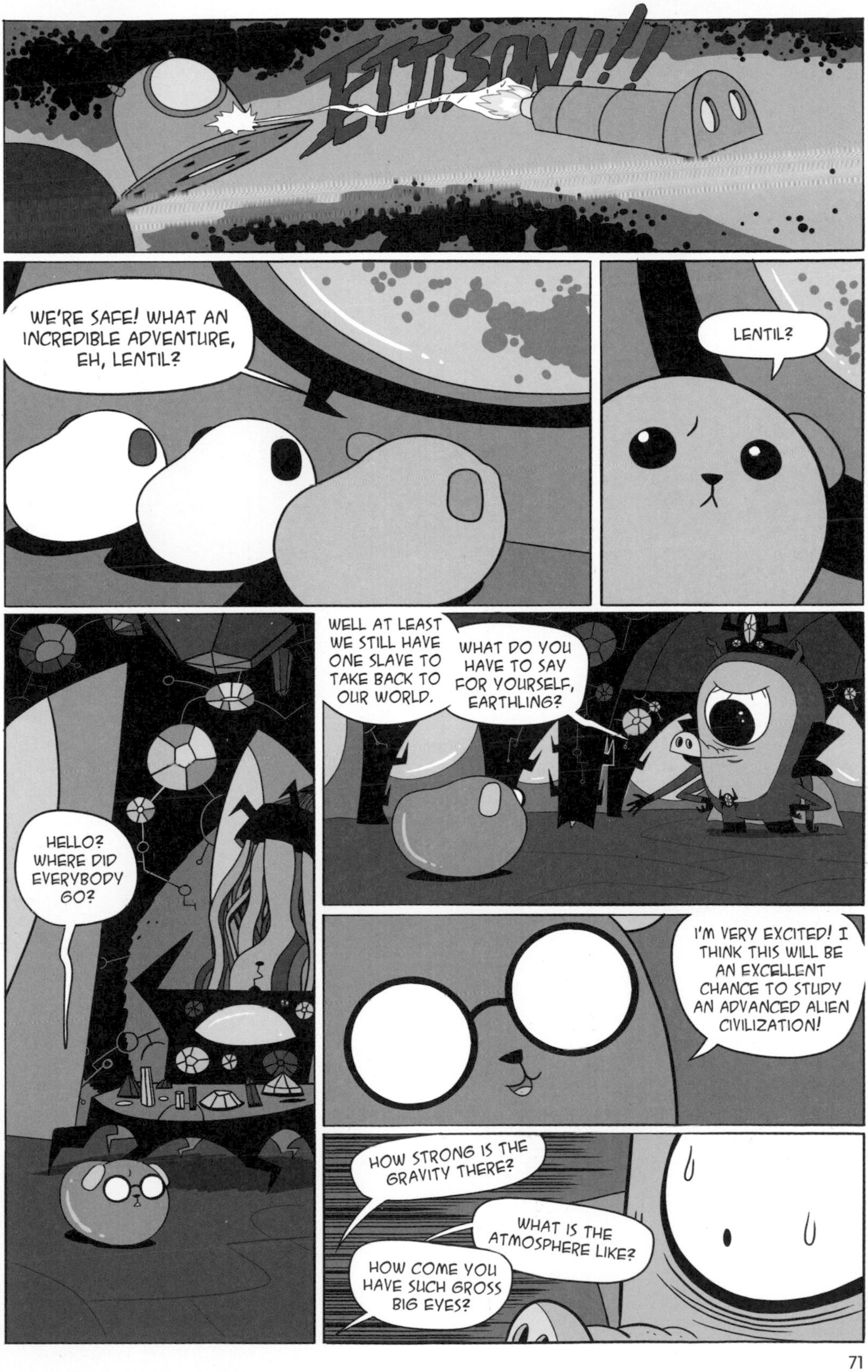
JETTISON!!!
WE'RE SAFE! WHAT AN INCREDIBLE ADVENTURE, EH, LENTIL?
LENTIL?
HELLO? WHERE DID EVERYBODY GO?
WELL AT LEAST WE STILL HAVE ONE SLAVE TO TAKE BACK TO OUR WORLD.
WHAT DO YOU HAVE TO SAY FOR YOURSELF, EARTHLING?
I'M VERY EXCITED! I THINK THIS WILL BE AN EXCELLENT CHANCE TO STUDY AN ADVANCED ALIEN CIVILIZATION!
HOW STRONG IS THE GRAVITY THERE?
WHAT IS THE ATMOSPHERE LIKE?
HOW COME YOU HAVE SUCH GROSS BIG EYES?

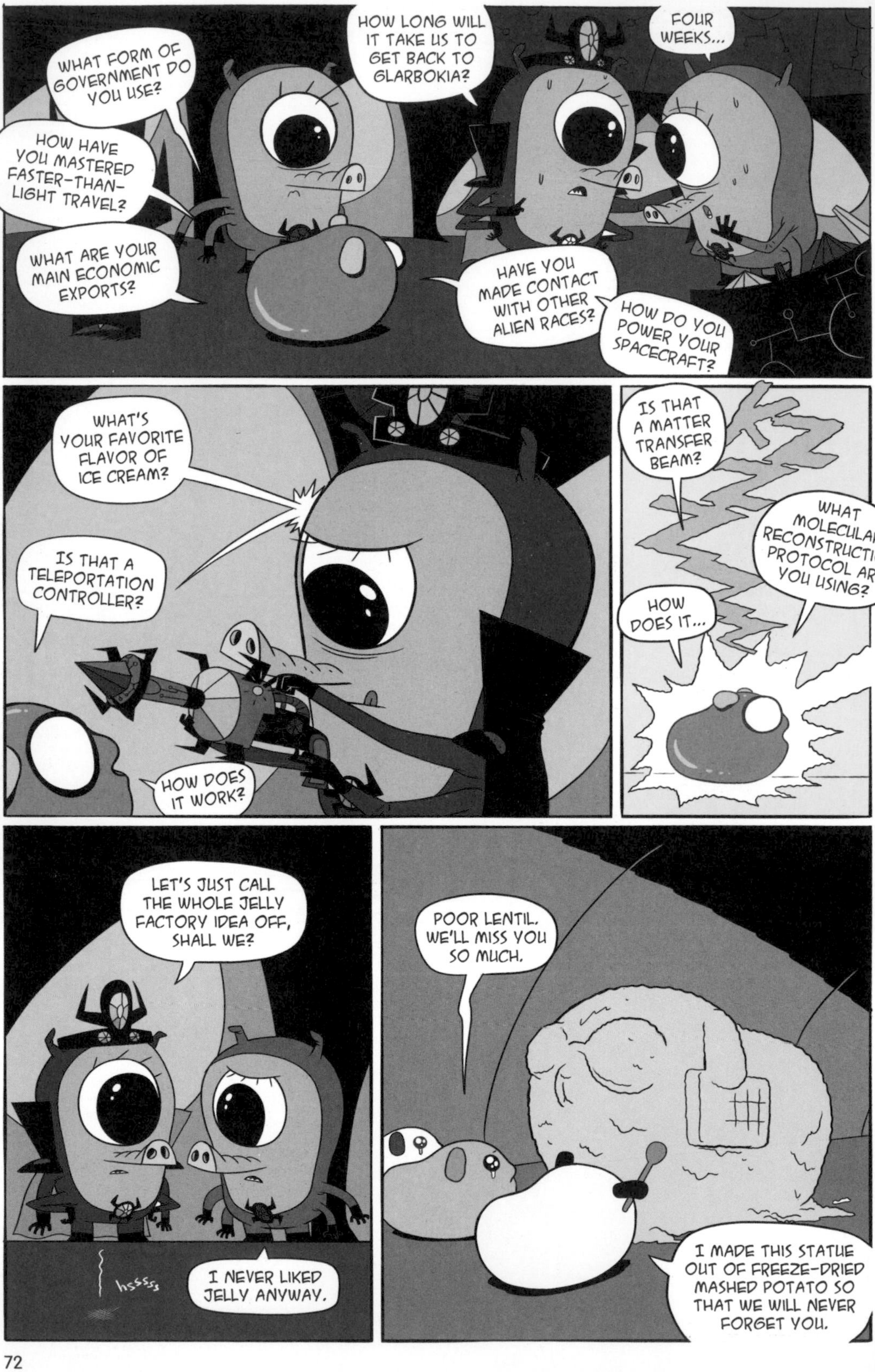
WHAT FORM OF GOVERNMENT DO YOU USE?
HOW HAVE YOU MASTERED FASTER-THAN-LIGHT TRAVEL?
WHAT ARE YOUR MAIN ECONOMIC EXPORTS?
HOW LONG WILL IT TAKE US TO GET BACK TO GLARBOKIA?
HAVE YOU MADE CONTACT WITH OTHER ALIEN RACES?
FOUR WEEKS...
HOW DO YOU POWER YOUR SPACECRAFT?
WHAT'S YOUR FAVORITE FLAVOR OF ICE CREAM?
IS THAT A TELEPORTATION CONTROLLER?
HOW DOES IT WORK?
IS THAT A MATTER TRANSFER BEAM?
WHAT MOLECULAR RECONSTRUCTIO PROTOCOL ARE YOU USING?
HOW DOES IT...
LET'S JUST CALL THE WHOLE JELLY FACTORY IDEA OFF, SHALL WE?
hsssss
I NEVER LIKED JELLY ANYWAY.
POOR LENTIL. WE'LL MISS YOU SO MUCH.
I MADE THIS STATUE OUT OF FREEZE-DRIED MASHED POTATO SO THAT WE WILL NEVER FORGET YOU.

MATERIALIZE

WHAT AN EXTRAORDINARY EXPERIENCE!

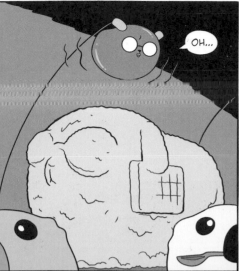

OH...

SQUELCH!

YAY! LENTIL! YOU ESCAPED!

AND YOU WOULD GO VERY NICELY WITH GRAVY!

NOW THAT WE'RE ALL SAFE, I CAN FLY US BACK TO EARTH...

OH NO, IT'S DEFINITELY MY TURN TO FLY! NO ONE FLIES BACK TO EARTH BETTER THAN ME.

SIGH. SURE CRANBERRY, GO AHEAD.

NOW, WHERE'S THE "FLY BACK TO EARTH" BUTTON?

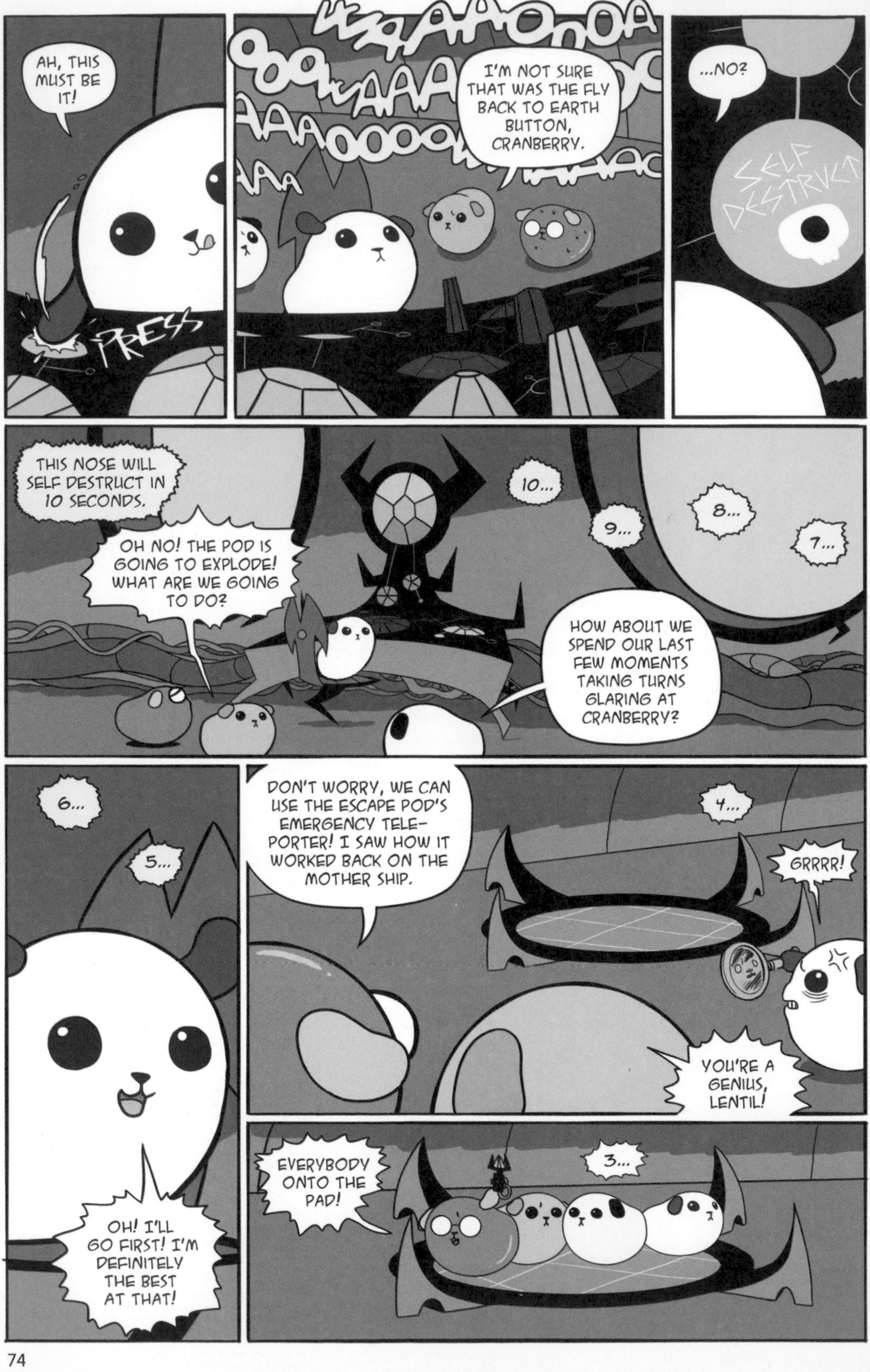

AH, THIS MUST BE IT!
PRESS
I'M NOT SURE THAT WAS THE FLY BACK TO EARTH BUTTON, CRANBERRY.
...NO?
SELF DESTRUCT
THIS NOSE WILL SELF DESTRUCT IN 10 SECONDS.
10...
OH NO! THE POD IS GOING TO EXPLODE! WHAT ARE WE GOING TO DO?
9...
8...
7...
HOW ABOUT WE SPEND OUR LAST FEW MOMENTS TAKING TURNS GLARING AT CRANBERRY?
6...
5...
OH! I'LL GO FIRST! I'M DEFINITELY THE BEST AT THAT!
DON'T WORRY, WE CAN USE THE ESCAPE POD'S EMERGENCY TELE-PORTER! I SAW HOW IT WORKED BACK ON THE MOTHER SHIP.
4...
GRRRR!
YOU'RE A GENIUS, LENTIL!
EVERYBODY ONTO THE PAD!
3...

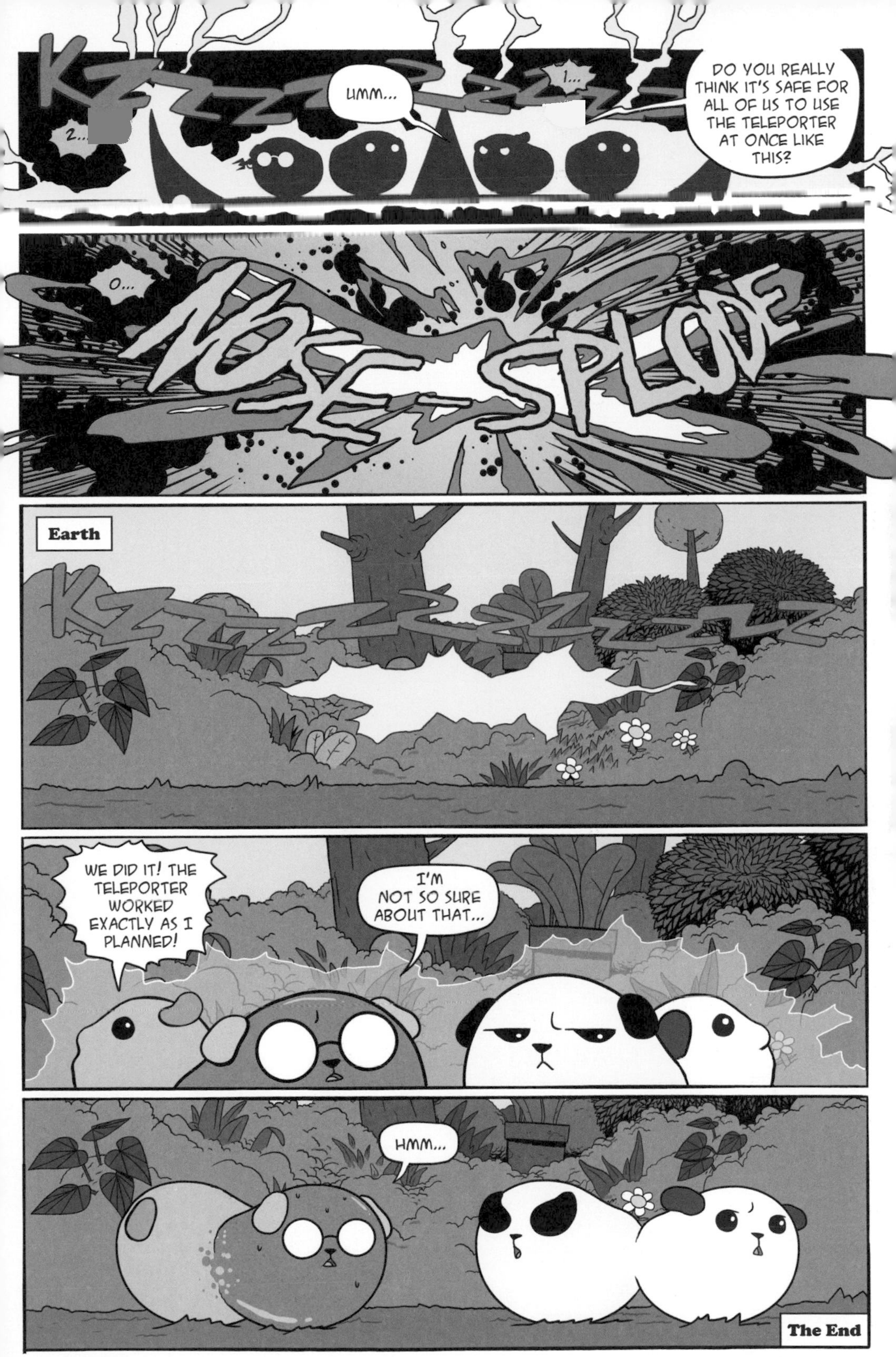
2...
UMM...
1...
DO YOU REALLY THINK IT'S SAFE FOR ALL OF US TO USE THE TELEPORTER AT ONCE LIKE THIS?
0...
Earth
WE DID IT! THE TELEPORTER WORKED EXACTLY AS I PLANNED!
I'M NOT SO SURE ABOUT THAT...
HMM...
The End

mameshiba

On the
LOOSE!

HOW TO BE A WINNER! WITH CRANBERRY BEAN

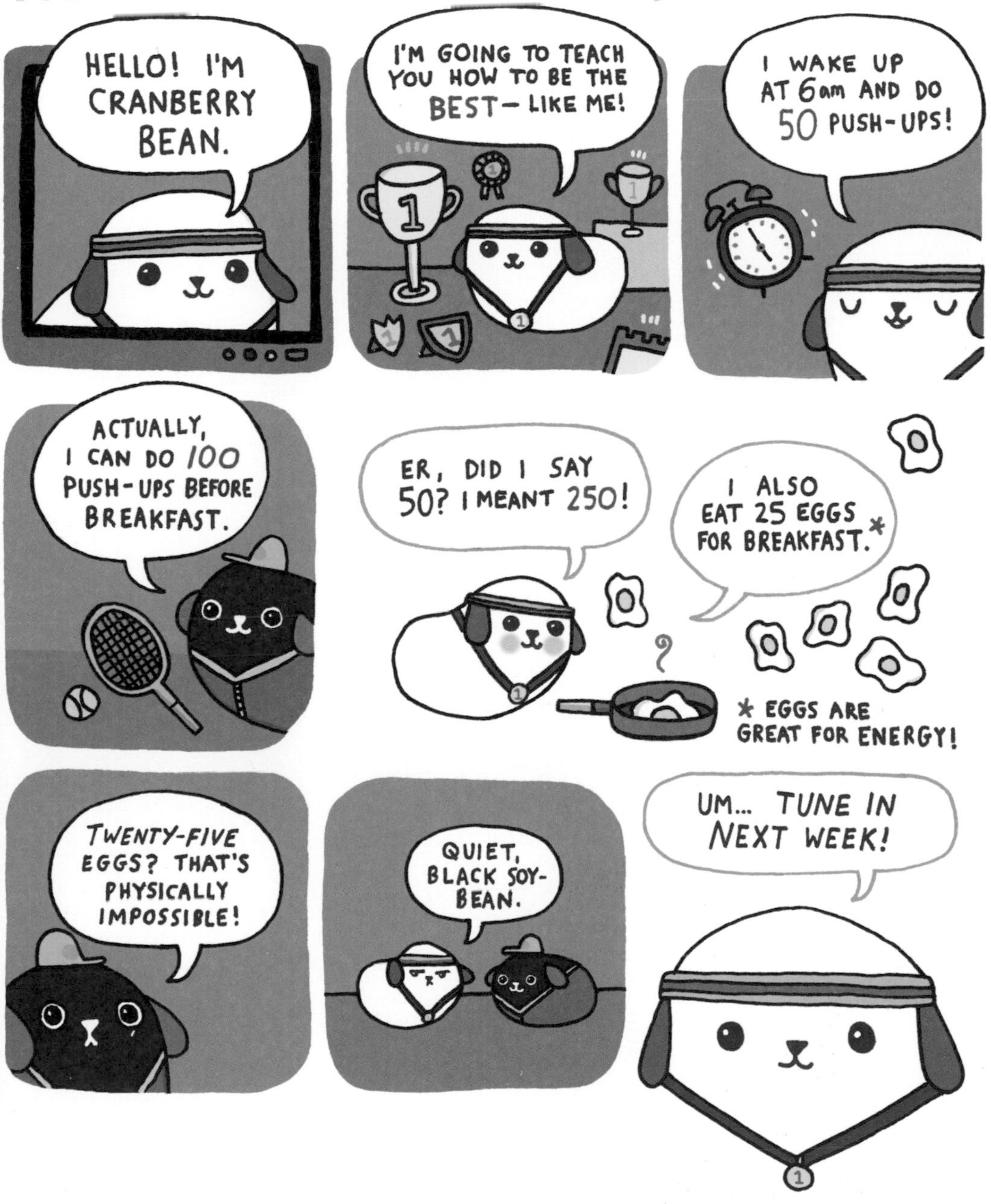
HELLO! I'M CRANBERRY BEAN.
I'M GOING TO TEACH YOU HOW TO BE THE BEST— LIKE ME!
I WAKE UP AT 6am AND DO 50 PUSH-UPS!
ACTUALLY, I CAN DO 100 PUSH-UPS BEFORE BREAKFAST.
ER, DID I SAY 50? I MEANT 250!
I ALSO EAT 25 EGGS FOR BREAKFAST.*
* EGGS ARE GREAT FOR ENERGY!
TWENTY-FIVE EGGS? THAT'S PHYSICALLY IMPOSSIBLE!
QUIET, BLACK SOY-BEAN.
UM... TUNE IN NEXT WEEK!

THE END.

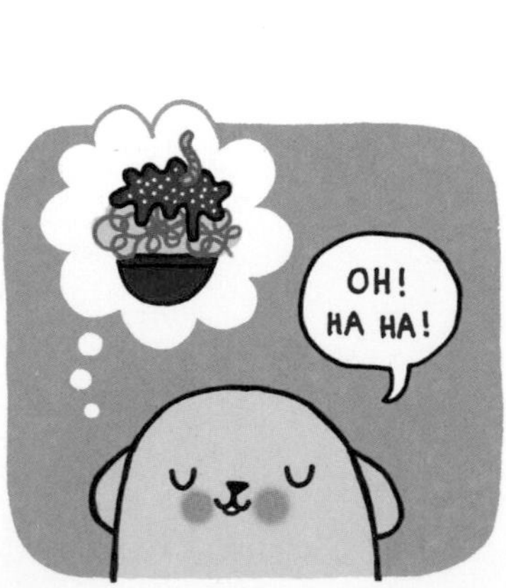
OH!
HA HA!

Look for more
Mameshiba adventures
COMING SOON!

james turner

started making comics as soon as he was first able to hold a pencil, and has been spouting a nonsensical whirlwind of monsters, robots and talking vegetables ever since. His acclaimed web comic *The Unfeasible Adventures of Beaver and Steve* won tens of thousands of followers online, and his anthropomorphic crime fighting team "The Super Animal Adventure Squad" appeared weekly in the pages of the children's comic the DFC. He has sworn that he will not stop making comics until every bizarre character, every unfeasible adventure, and every terrible pun has been uncovered. But he might stop for a bit if someone offers him a biscuit.

jorge monlongo

Monlongoshiba's natural habitat is Madrid, Spain. It eats all sorts of things and likes to sleep late. It can sometimes be seen drawing comic books, illustrating books or painting, but usually it just likes hanging out and being lazy. To learn more about Monlongoshiba, visit **monlongo.com**.

gemma correll

is a freelance illustrator, coffee drinker and sometime ukelele player, based in deepest, darkest England. She has exhibited her work in galleries and shop windows around the world and her artwork has been reproduced on everything from placemats to t-shirts to umbrellas. She has also had her work published in various books, annuals and magazines.

Gemma dreams of one day owning a house somewhere warm, with a mezzanine, pretty curtains and space for several small squishy-faced dogs and a few fluffy kitties.

Original Mameshiba characters created and designed by:
Sukwon Kim

Original Mameshiba art direction by:
Shoko Watanabe

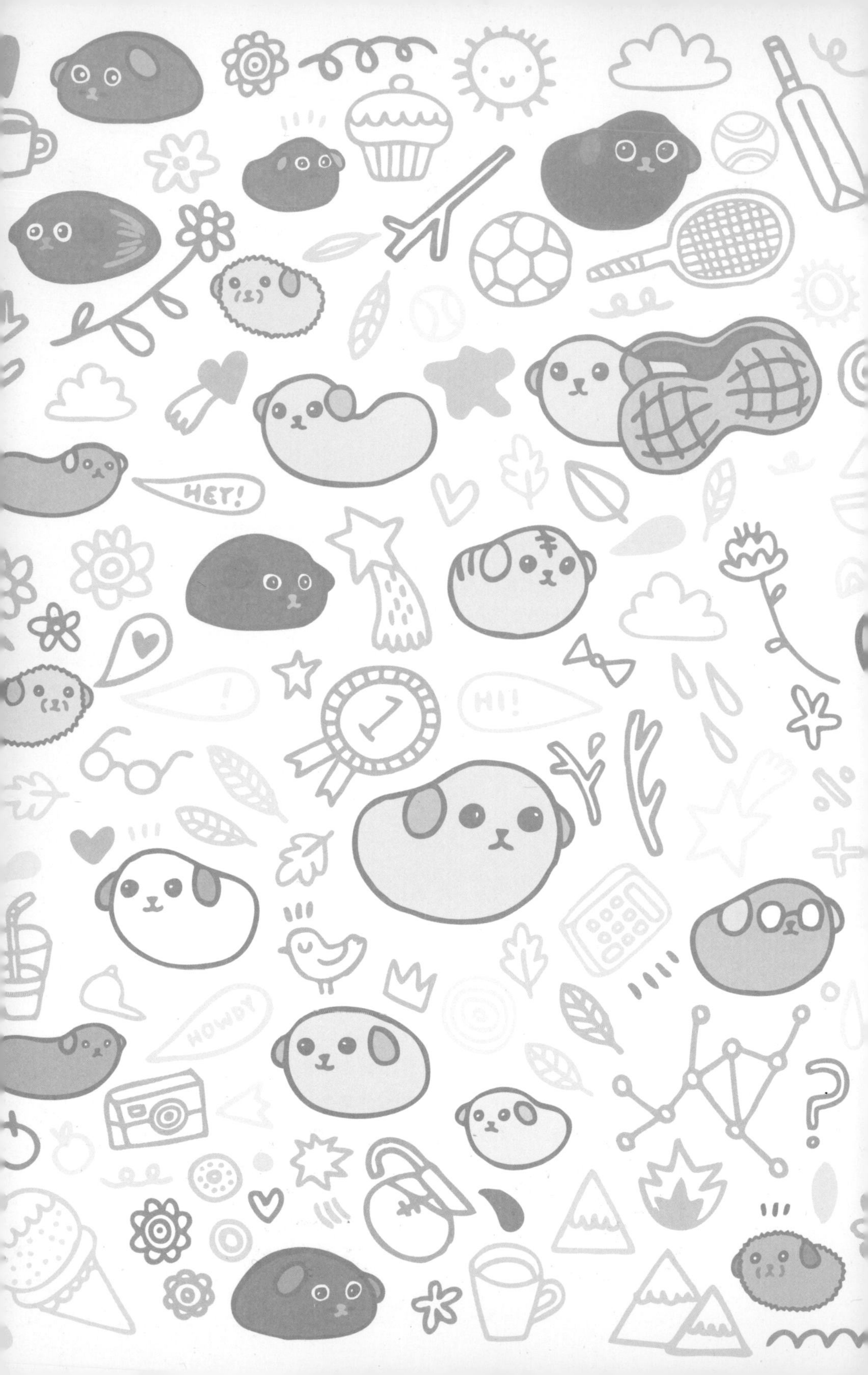
HEY!
HI!
HOWDY